Luke's Redemption

Reading Order

Big River Pack:
Gray's Wolf
Micah's Match
Emory's Mate
Reed's Girl
Tristan's Voice

Blackwater Bears:
Colton's Kitty
Noah's Fire
Carter's Devotion
Luke's Redemption

Luke's Redemption

Lynn Howard

@2019

Published by Twisted Heart Press, LLC

ALL RIGHTS RESERVED: No part of this book may be reproduced, stored in a retrieval system, or transmitted, in any form or by any means, without the prior permission in writing of the publisher, nor be otherwise circulated in any form of binding or cover other than that in which it is published and without a similar condition including this condition being imposed on the subsequent purchaser. Your non-refundable purchase allows you to one legal copy of this work for your own personal use. You do not have resell or distribution rights without the prior written permission of both the publisher and copyright owner of this book. This book cannot be copied in any format, sold, or otherwise transferred from your computer to another through upload, or for a fee.

Disclaimer: This book may contain explicit sexual content, graphic, adult language, and situations that some readers may find objectionable. This e-book is for sale to adults ONLY, as defined by the laws of the country in which you made your purchase. Lynn Howard will not be responsible for any loss, harm, injury or death resulting from use of the information contained in any of its titles.

This is a work of fiction. All characters, places, businesses, and incidents are from the author's imagination. Any resemblance to actual places, people, or events is purely coincidental. Any trademarks mentioned herein are not authorized by the trademark owners and do not in any way mean the work is sponsored by or associated with the trademark owners. Any trademarks used are specifically in a descriptive capacity.

Acknowledgments

I have to thank my beautiful betas, Linda, Christina, and Brei-Ayn. And a huge thank you to my beautiful editor/therapist, Genevieve Scholl. These books would suck without your input and keen eyes. Love you!

To the readers: I can't believe how good you all are to me and my characters. With your support, there will be even more books in the world of these sexy, country boy Shifters.

And to my family: Thank you for always listening to my crazy rambling, for supporting me through my writing journey, and making sure my coffee mug is always full.

Prologue

Piper hefted her bags from the cart into the trunk of her car. The air was turning cooler as summer began its farewells. It would still be a few more weeks before the days grew shorter and the leaves would drop, but the threat of autumn was in the damp wind kicking up her hair and whipping it around her face.

She blamed that wind for not seeing what was coming. She blamed that wind for her temporary blindness. That was the only way her brother had caught her off guard.

Piper had spent the last few months watching over her shoulder any time she was away from watching eyes. It was the times when she was most vulnerable – at home, in her yard at night, or, like tonight, in an empty parking lot when the sun had gone down – that her brother preferred to attack her. It was like he wanted her to know she was never safe.

Before she had the chance to drop into her car or even duck, Barret's fist made contact with the side of her head, knocking her against the driver's side door.

Stars danced in Piper's vision as she righted herself and planted her feet shoulder width apart. She might not be able to match her oldest brother in strength, but at least she could try to keep him from knocking her to the ground. It was always worse when she was on the ground. He could use his feet along with his fists to punish her.

"What are you doing?" Piper asked, trying her best to keep the fear out of her voice.

"Time's up, little sister," he said.

Before she could ask anymore questions, Barrett's fist flew again. She threw her arms up, blocking her face, but it only lasted a moment. The blow to the side of her head knocked her to the side. She had to choose whether she wanted to keep her hands covering her face or use them to stop herself from hitting the ground.

Piper tried to push herself up, tried to get her feet under her, tried for her solid stance, but that last hit had rattled her brain and knocked her senseless. A kick to her stomach had Piper doubled over and dropping to the stomach as she gasped for air.

"What…do you want?" Piper asked. At that moment, she would've agreed to almost anything. Except returning home. That she couldn't do. Although, the pain she felt radiating from her head and now her stomach might make her change her mind.

Barrett didn't answer her. Just waited until she rolled to her back and slammed his fist against her face, catching her cheek right below her eye socket when she tried to flinch away.

She hurt. Everything hurt. And she couldn't think straight.

Barrett lunged for her again, his fist balled up, an evil glint in his eyes.

And then he was gone. It was like wind had blown him away.

Now, all she could see was the broad back of a man. His shoulders raised and fell with deep, angry breaths. Piper could smell fur from where she laid in the fetal position on the ground. Who was he? Where the hell had he come from?

"You piece of shit," the man growled out, his voice deep and gravelly. He was trembling. It was obvious the stranger was a Shifter; was he on the verge of losing control over his animal?

The guy stomped toward Barrett, or at least she assumed that was what he was doing. His big body blocked most of her vision. What wasn't blocked was lined with gray and twinkling stars. And not the pretty kind, either.

Barrett was mumbling something Piper couldn't make out and his voice sounded further away. After a few moments, the guy returned and knelt beside her.

His hand was warm and calloused as he ran it across her face, then moved her hair away to inspect the damage. His eyes. That she would never forget. His eyes were a warm, light brown. They reminded her of a glass of Jack Daniels whiskey. Bear Shifter, maybe? They all had brown eyes. And the Blackwater Clan resided nearby.

"Come on," he grumbled in that deep voice again. He gently slid a big arm behind her back and helped her sit up. "We need to leave before someone spots us and calls the cops."

He helped her to her feet and into her car. "Thank you," she said. Her face throbbed with the words.

"No problem." He looked over his shoulder as if watching for Barrett to return.

"I'm Piper," she said.

His head turned, his eyes flashed from whiskey brown to amber then back again. "Luke."

Piper nodded and then Luke pushed her door shut. He took a few steps back, his eyes watching the area, then climbed into his big, beat up truck. He waited a few minutes for her to pull out of the parking lot, but then his headlights were right behind her. And they stayed behind her until she pulled into her driveway.

As she pushed from the car, every movement sending pain signals to her muddled brain, she tensed when she caught a scent on the breeze. And then her body relaxed muscle by muscle and a sense of peace and calm came over her.

Luke was there. She couldn't see him, but even in her human form she picked up his scent. He was there to watch over her. She wasn't sure how she knew that, but she did. She'd never been more certain of anything in her life.

And that was the first night in over a year Piper slept more than four hours and didn't suffer a single nightmare. Because her bear was out there watching over her.

Chapter One

Luke paced the woods, staying deep enough in the trees that she wouldn't see or hear him. If she'd stepped out onto the concrete porch outside her front door, she might've caught a whiff of his scent. But he'd been careful the last few months to stay downwind to keep from scaring her.

This had become his nightly routine. He'd finish whatever he had to do at home, wait for the sun to start setting, then he'd drive close enough to her house and park his truck off the road so he could Shift in the woods and run the rest of the way to her house.

He felt like a stalker. But that wasn't what he was doing. Ever since he'd caught some dude slapping her around, he'd made it his personal mission to keep her safe. He'd beat the fuck out of the dude, chased him off, then followed her home. She'd thanked him for his help, that sweet, feminine voice tightening things in him he didn't want to think about, then hurried into the house. He'd waited until he'd heard the locks click into place before he'd left her driveway.

He hated that she lived so far off the beaten path. It was common for Shifters to avoid having neighbors, but they usually had a Clan, or Pack, or Pride to look after them.

Piper had no one.

False. She had Luke. Even if she didn't know it. He'd paced the woods, keeping his senses tuned to the forest around him, and headed off any threat. Including whoever that asshole at the grocery store had been. Who the fuck slaps around on a woman? Especially in public. In a grocery store parking lot, none the less.

A low life piece of shit, that was who. Luke had no idea who the man was to Piper, and it didn't matter. He'd keep her safe for as long as he could.

He was running on fumes lately. He'd stayed near her home until close to two or three in the morning, head back to his cabin for a quick shower, then sleep for a few hours before he had to go into work. He couldn't keep going like this. At least on the weekends he could sleep during the day. He felt like Piper was safer during the day, locked inside her own house.

And when she was at work. The woman actually worked at the library. What Shifter worked at a library? Although Emory from Big River Pack worked for a local farm supply store. And June, Carter's mate, used to work for a local pub and grill kind of place. But both women were in control of their animals. Most males weren't. At least most males he knew.

Memories of different Shifters going all furry while at Moe's, his Clan brother's bar, flitted through his head as he watched the lights turn off inside of Piper's.

Standing slowly, he lifted his snout and tilted his head when he watched her step outside. She didn't go many places after she got home from work. In fact, he'd only seen her leave once after work and that was to run to the grocery store.

Fuck. The fact he knew all that made him feel like even more of a stalker.

"Well?" Piper's voice floated on the breeze. "Do you want to come with me?"

Luke looked around the area, trying to figure out who she was talking to. When she began to walk closer to him, her light brown, shoulder length hair blowing in the breeze, he realized she was looking right at him.

Oh shit.

In a rush, Luke Shifted back into his human form, grunting from the pain of a quick Shift, and yanked on his clothes as fast as he could. He'd gotten good at tying them to his leg before heading over there. He didn't like the thought of fighting with his dick flopping in the wind if someone ever did show up.

Stepping out of the tree line, he stood a few feet from the woods and frowned at her.

"Do you want to come with me or did you want to stay out here all night?"

Fuck, he loved her voice. It was soft and feminine, but not at all girly. She propped her hands on her hips and Luke did everything he could to keep his eyes on her face so she wouldn't think he was ogling her. Of course, all he wanted to do was ogle her. He always watched her hips sway as she left her car and headed inside. He loved the way she tossed her hair over her shoulder while she was fiddling with her keys. He even loved her small, perky tits. They were small, but they'd fit in each of his hands.

Nope. Not thinking about that. He was there to keep her safe, not seduce her.

"Where are you going?" he asked, his voice scratchy from lack of use. He didn't talk to many people. He didn't hold conversations more than he had to. He hated to think about how much he'd let everyone down, especially Emory.

"I'm hungry. I need to go to the grocery store. I figured you could ride along instead of sitting out here all night."

"How did you know I was here?" he asked, narrowing his eyes.

"Oh please. I'm a Shifter, too. I have the same senses you do. You're not nearly as quiet as you think."

"You're not pissed?"

She crossed her arms and tilted her head. "Depends."

"On what?"

"Why are you out here? Are you hoping I'll leave a curtain open while changing?"

His dick thumped the back of his jeans at that thought. He pushed it away and thought about one of his buddies, anything to keep his hormones in check. "No. I wanted to make sure you were safe."

"It's been weeks."

She definitely remembered him. He liked that. But he didn't like the fact she knew he was outside her home and never said anything. How did she know he wasn't there to hurt her, too?

"I know," he said, crossing his arms like she did.

Piper chewed on her bottom lip. Luke couldn't help himself; his eyes went straight to her mouth. "I don't want a mate," she said.

"Neither do I."

"I don't want to be paired up."

"Neither do I," he repeated.

Her eyes narrowed again like she was trying to tell if he was lying. Not a lie. He had no desire to be tethered to someone, to be addicted to another person the way all his friends were. They'd all lost control of their own damn minds and bodies. None of them could go more than a few hours without touching their mates. And Luke got the joy of listening to all the lovemaking, day in and day out. He'd contemplated leaving Blackwater territory more than once. Hell, he'd contemplated it more than a dozen times.

Piper turned and headed toward her little Toyota. "You coming?" She looked at him over her shoulder as she lowered into the driver's seat.

Riding along with her to the grocery store was a bad idea. It was too domestic. It was too normal. He just wanted to keep her safe. He didn't want to fail another person.

He opened his mouth to reject the invitation and winced when the wrong words came out of his mouth. "Yes," he said as he pulled the passenger side door open.

Luke had to fold himself almost in half to get into the small car. While Piper wasn't nearly as small as a couple of the women from the Big River Pack, she was quite a bit smaller than he was. And petite. Fragile. Breakable.

He tried to keep his eyes straight ahead as she aimed the vehicle into Cedar Hill, but the traitorous fuckers kept cutting to the side to get a glimpse of her. Her thin arms, her thin, yet muscular legs, her thin fingers wrapped around the steering wheel. He suppressed a chuckle at the way she held the wheel at the ten and two the way they'd been taught as kids. And she drove under the speed limit, kept quite a bit of distance between the vehicle in front of her, and hesitated almost a full five seconds at stop signs and lights, even if there was no one in the cross section.

Piper was a cautious, nervous driver. And it was driving him up the wall.

Luke leaned to the side and checked her speed. Yep. Still going under. "You always drive like a grandma?" he said, attempting to tease her.

Her lips pursed and a tiny crease formed between her brows. "I haven't been driving that long. It still makes me nervous."

Luke turned his head to look at her, but she didn't look at him. She hadn't been driving that long? What did that mean? She looked somewhere in her mid to late twenties. She should've been driving for at least ten years.

Unless she was like the women in the lion Prides. But she wasn't a lion. He'd seen her Shift and run into the woods behind her house. Piper was a beautiful fawn colored cougar. He had to admit he didn't know much about cougar Prides or their relationship to females. And it'd only been a couple of years since he and his friends had battled for the rights of female Shifters. Maybe she'd only recently earned her freedom from an oppressive mate or family.

A wave of anger burned through his veins at the thought of her being mistreated, even if he hadn't known her then. He knew her now. And he'd met because she was being mistreated.

"Who was that guy?" he said, trying to swallow the growl trying to work from his chest.

"What guy?" she asked, her eyes still glued on the road. The sun had set and she had her brights on, but she was still leaning forward and squinting her eyes in concentration.

Luke frowned at her profile. "In the parking lot."

The damnedest thing happened; he swore he saw the moment she shut down, like a mask slammed into place. Her eyes even looked vacant as she shook her head side to side in the tiniest movement.

She wasn't going to answer. He could respect that. Yet he was still pissed. He wanted to know who the fucker was. Instead of hiding outside her house all night, every night, he could hunt the asshole down and make sure he never even thought about Piper again.

The rest of the ride was in silence, and not the comfortable kind he had with his Clan sisters, either. He could practically feel the anxiety rolling from her. And maybe a little fear. Of him? Of the question?

The parking lot was mostly empty when they pulled into the local mom and pop place. It wasn't that late, but Mondays tended to be slow everywhere in town. It was like people were still recovering from the weekend.

Piper turned the Toyota off and looked around the parking lot, even turned in her seat to look behind her as if she was checking to make sure no one was hiding in the shadows. When she was satisfied, she pushed open her door, clutched her bag to her side, and jogged toward the entrance. Luke stepped out and frowned after her. Did she forget he was with her? Did she really think he'd let anyone touch her as long as he was there?

Luke ambled inside, not bothering to rush in to catch her. The store wasn't very big; he'd find her easily, especially since there was hardly anyone there. And because he'd memorized every inch of her face and body over the last few weeks.

Groaning at his last thought and sneering at a yokel who looked his way, Luke went down the front aisle, looking down each until he located her. She was holding two cans of Raviolis in her hands, comparing the ingredients. By the look of her physique, she didn't need to worry about calorie content.

"What are you doing?"

She ghosted him with a glance then went back to reading the back. "Trying to find the one with the least amount of crap," she said, that sweet, soft voice sounding distracted.

"Pretty sure they're both made of crap."

With a sigh, she set them both on the shelves and pushed her cart further down the row. "I liked it better when I didn't know about artificial ingredients and preservatives and GMOs."

Luke couldn't help the huff of surprised laughter. He followed her around the store, one eye on her, the other on their surroundings. It was one thing to be in her territory, it was completely different to be right back at the place she'd been assaulted. She seemed to feel safer with him at her side. Or maybe it was inside the grocery store with other witnesses.

He liked the idea of it being *him* better.

Piper didn't buy much, just a lot of frozen pizzas, some apples, and a half gallon of milk. Her cheeks flushed pink as they went down the personal hygiene area. "Would you mind running back and grabbing me a package of bacon?"

Luke looked around and realized she needed girl stuff and was too embarrassed to grab it with him standing there. He'd never admit it to her – or anyone else – but he'd bought those things for Shawnee, Hollyn, and even June on a few occasions.

Doing as she asked, Luke took his time getting the bacon, then found her near the registers. There wasn't much in her cart. By the way she'd said she needed to go to the store, he'd figured she had an empty fridge. Or maybe she'd just been craving.

Or maybe, even though she'd said she didn't want to be paired up, she'd found an excuse to lure him out of the woods.

No. That was stupid. And something he didn't need to think about. He hadn't been lying when he said he didn't want a mate. He only wanted to make sure she, and every other female he knew, was safe.

Groceries bagged and hooked over Luke's arms, he followed Piper back out to her car.

She sat in the driver's seat, the engine running but she wasn't pulling out of the parking lot.

"My brother," she said so softly Luke had almost missed it.

He turned and frowned at her. "That asshole was your brother?"

She dipped her head once but wouldn't meet his eyes.

Why the fuck would her own brother treat her like that? Who would treat their tiny sister like that? Who would treat any woman like that? He knew the answer to that; he'd seen it so many times through the years, including in his own fucking family.

"Where is he now?" Luke asked and, this time, was unable to hold back the growl.

This time, Piper turned her head to look at him, stared at him as if she were going over something in her head. After a few silent moments, she shook her head and put the car in reverse. "You can't stop him, Luke. You can't stop any of them."

"Any of who?"

She kept shaking her head side to side, her lips clamped together.

"Any of who, Piper?" he pushed harder.

"Luke, I appreciate everything you've done, but it's time for you to go back to your own life. The longer this goes on, the worse it'll get." She sounded so sad and so resigned to whatever was supposed to happen to her.

Well, fuck that. Nothing would happen to her, not as long as he could do something about it.

But what did she mean? What did she mean by it'll get worse the longer it goes on?

"Am I making things worse, Piper?" he pushed out through a closing throat. Leaving her to the evil hands of her brother went against everything he stood for. He couldn't live with yet another failure.

She swallowed audibly and nodded her head in jerky movements.

"What's going on? Why was he doing that?"

Piper flipped on her blinker and turned onto the deserted road where Luke parked his car. How the hell had she known where it was? Why had she waited so long to let him know she knew he was out there?

She pulled her car behind his and put it into park. "I appreciate what you're trying to do. I just wanted to tell you that. I appreciate what you did…that night. But, please, forget I exist. It's best for both us."

When she turned her face toward his, he was gutted. There was so much sadness in her green eyes it broke his heart. He'd do anything to make her smile, to make her feel better, to end whatever made her look so lonely and desperate.

A hundred replies went through his head, but he didn't say any of them. He wanted to keep her safe, but what if he was making her life harder?

"If you ever need me…" And he let that sentence hang in the air. Her phone was sitting in the cup holder. He picked it up and programmed his number into her phone, then put it back. "I don't care what time it is. Or what's going on. Call me and I'll be there."

Then he pushed from the car and walked to his truck like his body was full of concrete, each step heavy.

With one hand on his open door, he held the other up to shield his eyes from her headlights and watched her back away and disappear down the two-lane road.

"Fuck!" he bellowed into the quiet evening.

He was tempted to punch the side of his truck. Wasn't like anyone would notice a new dent in his POS. But he balled his hands into fists and climbed into his truck, gripping the wheel so hard his knuckles popped, and rested his head against the cool faux leather.

What was he supposed to do? Keep hanging out in the woods outside her house for the rest of his life? He could always hunt down this fuckwad of a brother and beat the piss out of him and make him see Luke's side of all of this.

For the first time since he'd found Piper cowering, her arms raised to defend her face from the fist flying at her, he was tempted to go to his Clan for help. Carter would know what to do. And if he didn't, he could talk to the other Alphas and get their take on it. After all, people like Piper was who they'd fought for a couple years back. What was happening to Piper was against Shifter law. Wasn't it?

In reality, he had no idea what exactly what was going on. And Piper had pretty much told him to stay away. Without more details, his fucking hands were tied.

Sitting up, Luke threw his truck into gear with a little too much force and aimed it for home. Colton and Shawnee were outside on their porch and frowned at his arrival.

"You're home early," Colton said, his usual friendly smirk on his stupid face.

Luke grunted in response.

"Everything okay? Something we can help with?" Shawnee called after Luke as he hurried to his cabin.

He raised his hand, both waving her off and bidding her goodnight. He could blast his brothers, but he could never be mean to Shawnee. Her spirit was still broken, even if she had healed more than anyone could've ever expected since arriving in Blackwater.

Luke loved Shawnee. And Hollyn. And June. He might not tell them, but he did. They were just as much his family as their mates were. But affection had never come easy to him.

His place was dark when he walked through the door, but he didn't bother turning on any of the lights. It wasn't like he needed them to see. Even in the dark, he saw everything as if it were a cloudy day. And for some reason, the thought of filling the rooms with the warm light of the lamps felt…wrong. He didn't feel warm. He felt cold inside. And empty. And fucking irate.

Luke plopped his ass on his couch and stared at the dark television set and pictured Piper's face. He pictured the first time he saw her with so much fear and pain in her eyes. He pictured her coming home from the library after work. He pictured her the moment she called him out of the woods. And then he pictured the pained look on her face just before he got out of her vehicle.

Dragging a hand down his face, he growled deep and low and dropped his head back against the cushion. What the fuck was he supposed to do now? He'd become so obsessed over guarding her he'd almost forgotten what life was like before he'd found her. It wasn't like he could forget about her.

Giving up on relaxing, he stormed outside and straight over to the steps of Colton's porch.

"There's this woman. A Shifter. I was at the store and came outside to find some dude wailing on her. No one stopped him or even seemed to notice. So I knocked the fuck out of the guy. And I've been hanging outside her house for weeks to keep her safe. But she knew I was out there and told me to go shopping with her then told me to go home. It was her brother. Her own fucking brother was the asshole beating her up. And she said if I stay there it'll get worse. And I don't know how the fuck to walk away from this."

He inhaled deeply after spilling everything. Colton and Shawnee gaped at him, their eyes wide, their mouths hanging open.

"I don't think I've ever heard you say so many words at one time," Shawnee said in awe. She turned to her mate with his brows raised.

"Wow, dude," Colton said in that Tennessee accent. "Okay...uhhh." He turned toward Shawnee, mimicking her with his brows raised to his hairline. "Have you told any of this to Carter?"

"Does it sound like I've told it to anyone?" Luke growled out, his hands on his hips. He dropped his head and huffed out a frustrated breath. "What the fuck do I do? I can't just leave her to that asshole's fists. But she said me being around will make it worse."

"How would it make it worse?" Shawnee asked.

Head still hanging, Luke shook it. "I don't know. She wouldn't say. She didn't say much. Other than to tell me to hit the bricks."

"Is she your mate?" Shawnee asked, and damn it if it didn't sound like there was a smile in her voice.

Luke raised his head just enough to look at the redhead. "Don't start," he said. "I'm not looking for a mate. I'm just trying to keep her safe."

"You can't protect every single person on the planet," Shawnee said, her brows pulled together with a sad smile on her pink lips.

A growl rattled up his throat and escaped his lips before he could stop it. He needed to Shift. He needed to run. He needed to get some of this angry energy out before he lashed out at his own fucking Clan.

Turning his back on Shawnee and Colton, he pulled his shirt over his head and pushed his jeans down to his ankles as he crunched across the gravel.

"You want me to run with you, brother?" Colton called out.

Luke didn't answer, didn't confirm or deny him. Just let his bear have his body. The second his massive paws hit the ground he took off at a full run. He didn't know where he was going. He just needed to run. He needed to force the thought of Piper out of his head.

He needed to pretend he'd never laid eyes on that angel of a woman.

Chapter Two

Piper looked through the gap in her curtains for the fifteenth time since she'd gotten home. Luke was gone. He'd listened to her and left her property. She'd loved having him there, but every day he was there her family got more and more pissed. A wry smile stretched her lips when she thought about how scared of Luke her brother was. Barret might be tough when it came to a woman who was almost half his size, but when he came up against someone as big and strong and brave as Luke, he tucked his tail between his legs and ran.

Her heart hurt. Her heart hurt for so many reasons. Why couldn't she have a normal family? Why couldn't they love her the way she was? Why couldn't they follow the damn laws? Technically, they were. They simply found ways to skirt the edges and fly through the loopholes.

The buzzing across the room made her wince. She was getting yet another warning text telling her to lose the bear. They must not have tried to wander into her area if they didn't know Luke was already gone. And while she should probably tell them she'd run him off, she decided to have at least one more night of peace.

Pulling the curtains closed tightly, Piper shuffled to her bedroom and changed into her pajamas. Her pajamas consisted of a pair of leggings and a t-shirt along with a pair of shoes she left sitting beside her bed. She always felt the need to be ready. Ready to run, ready to fight, ready for whatever.

Curling onto her side, Piper allowed her mind to wander to Luke. She hadn't really remembered what he'd looked like from the night in the parking lot; her brain had been in fight or flight mode and panic had caused her brain to blur out quite a few details of that night. But Luke was handsome, almost pretty, but in a rugged, manly kind of way.

Luke's eyes were the color of whiskey, his lashes so long and dark, but the stubble on his cheeks and jaw along with the scar running down the left side of his face made him look dangerous. It was an intoxicating mix.

Piper's body grew tight and warm at the memory of his broad shoulders, his barrel chest, the tattoos that ran down his arms onto his hands. She wondered how much of his body was covered in the ink.

No. She didn't need to think about that kind of stuff. She had no desire to be paired up or mated. Hence the reason her family was constantly attacking her. They figured if they wore her down, she'd be more open to the arranged marriage they'd planned for her since her birth. The male they'd chosen for her wasn't unattractive, but his personality left a lot to be desired. He had no sense of humor, was misogynistic and could be cruel. And he had plans to be Alpha of her family Pride. Since Piper was the daughter of the current Alpha, everyone assumed she had no other choice.

Whatever. That wasn't the life she wanted. Hell. She hated even being in that Pride. She hated everything they stood for. She hated the way the way they treated other groups of Shifters. She hated the way they still saw females as nothing more than vessels for the next generation of fighters.

Sleep eluded her for hours. Her brain played on a loop, her memories of her childhood, that last beating she got from her big brother, the moment he'd been jerked away from her, the hulking figure who'd stood over her to guard her until Barret was gone. And then the moment Luke had stepped out of the tree line, his swagger full of masculinity and confidence. And sex appeal.

Just because she didn't want to be paired up didn't mean she couldn't fool around with the big bear, did it?

Of course it did. If her family found out Luke was not only still hanging around but sleeping with Piper on a regular basis, her punishment would only get worse.

Eventually, she did fall asleep, but it was nightmare filled and fitful. She'd be a zombie all day at work.

At least she didn't have to do manual labor or anything that could cause injury to someone else because her brain was mush.

Throwing her blankets off, she stood and immediately put the bed back in order, arranging the throw pillows at a perfect angle with the walls. She then made her way into the shower and scrubbed and shaved everything. Makeup and hair done and perfect, she rifled through her clothes and pulled out a pair of slacks, a blouse, and a pink cardigan. She was the stereotypical librarian, but she didn't care. She liked her clothes. With the exception of her family's pressures, she loved her life.

Picking a pair of black Mary Janes, she sat on her couch and slipped them on her feet. She wasn't even hungry. The thought of eating her morning oatmeal made her stomach turn. Instead, she rifled through the alphabetically stored granola bars until she found what she was looking for, tossed it into her purse, then headed out to her impeccably clean Toyota.

What would Luke think if he knew about her incessant need for order? And not just in her car and home, but her life. She hated messes. She hated chaos. She hated surprises. She preferred to know what would happen day to day, hour to hour, minute to minute. She liked to know where everything was at all times. A place for everything and everything in its place and all that.

Piper was the first one at the library. As usual. She liked to be early, liked the quiet solitude and the smell of the books first thing in the morning. She tossed her purse into the back room, then set about turning on the lights and firing up the computers. It was time to start the day. She needed to focus on something other than her family, Luke, and the punishment she knew was coming the second Barret and her parents realized she no longer had a bodyguard staying on her property.

Nope. Couldn't think about that. She'd just swing by Walgreens after work and pick up some more makeup and concealer. She'd need it.

As if she'd earned some kind of blessing, the day dragged on and she was even asked to work someone else's shift. Therefore, she got to be at the library for almost ten hours before clocking out. And then she made her way to the guillotine. Or at least that's how it felt. She felt as if she were delivering herself into the hands of her punisher.

And as if she'd conjured him her thoughts, Piper groaned when she spotted Barret's jeep parked in her driveway. She knew he'd be inside waiting for her. He, along with every single member of her Pride, had a key to her house. Not her choice. Even if they came by for a visit and a quick threat, they always made a mess, as if taunting her.

"Hey," she said to Barret who was sprawled on her floral couch, his dirty boots propped up on her whitewashed coffee table. She'd have to scrub the crap out of that when he left. Why would anyone think putting dirty work boots on white furniture was a good idea?

She toed her shoes off at the door and carried them to her closet where she lined them up with the rest of her color-coded shoes.

It wasn't that she was a clean freak, she merely liked order. It gave her peace.

"Where's the bear?" Barret asked while she was still hiding in her closet, folding her cardigan and slipping it into the hamper.

"Don't know," she said. She had to stop hiding, stop stalling, and face the music.

"Make yourself some new friends?" he asked, studying the label on the Heineken he'd pulled from her fridge. He didn't even ask permission, just took whatever the hell he wanted when he wanted. Like every other male in her Pride.

Piper knew about Luke and his Clan and the wolves from Big River Pack. She knew about the new laws. Even knew about the Hope Pride one of the former members of Big River had started for women like her. Women who didn't want to be forced into mating. Women who didn't want a life of oppression.

"No." She stood in the doorway of her bedroom and was tempted to go back into her closet and lock the door. Yes. She had a lock on the inside of her closet. Not that it would keep Barret out. But it made her feel as if she had a little control over the situation.

His eyes roamed her body. "I thought mom told you to eat more."

Piper looked down at her rail thin body. She was shapeless. Had the body of a boy. Had no breasts. Or that's what she'd been told since she'd hit puberty. It didn't matter how much she ate; she never gained weight. And it wasn't like ten more pounds would give her bigger boobs.

"I am," she said, fighting the urge to shuffle her feet under her brother's scrutiny. "I even bought some bacon and full fat milk last night."

"With the bear."

Her eyes jerked up to his face in surprise.

"You think we didn't know? You really think mom and dad didn't have someone watching you?"

"And you don't find any of that…sick? Or twisted?"

Barret chuckled but there was no humor to the sound. Nor did his grin reach his eyes. She wasn't even sure Barret knew how to smile in earnest. She wasn't sure anyone in her Pride knew how to smile. And if she were honest with herself, she wasn't sure *she'd* ever truly smiled. Or been happy.

That last thought sent sadness crashing into heart with so much force it took her breath.

"Have a seat," Barret said, patting the cushion beside him.

She might be scared and weak, but she wasn't stupid.

Piper crossed her living room and sat at the pretty Formica table that sat centered in her makeshift dining room. Really, it was just the space off her kitchen that she designated as her place to eat.

Crossing her legs at the knees, she folded her arms over her chest and waited for Barret to say whatever he had to say.

Barret leaned forward, his elbows resting on his knees. "Dad said you have two choices: mate with Andrew or come home and wait for him to choose someone else."

"I want a third choice," she said, keeping her eyes on the spot near Barret's feet. She couldn't make herself look him in the eye. She knew she was weak. *He* knew she was weak. And he'd definitely see it in her eyes.

Unfortunately, her avoidance of eye contact reminded Barret just how submissive Piper was.

Barret stood and walked slowly, doing his best to appear intimidating and menacing. He really didn't need to; she was damn near trembling with fear.

Lifting her head, she finally looked into Barret's face.

"What's your third choice?" he asked, a jerky smirk on his jerky face.

"How about I stay here, live my life the way I want, and don't bother anyone."

He threw his head back and laughed. When he dropped his head to look at her again, the smile was gone.

"Dad said you have a week to decide." He looked around her small house. "I'm sure Andrew wouldn't mind living in this shack."

That irritated Piper. Her place was not a shack. It was small, sure, but she was a small person living alone. The two-bedroom place was plenty big for her. It was cute and decorated exactly the way she wanted. If Andrew moved in, he'd change everything. He'd mess the place up and expect her to wait on him hand and foot and spread her legs at his command.

Barret stared down at her long enough she shifted her weight on the chair and began to fidget. He made her nervous. Everyone made her nervous.

Except Luke. She'd felt one hundred percent safe and comfortable with him. She never worried he'd hurt her or force her into anything. He just wanted to be her friend. Well, maybe not her friend. But still...

"One week." His hand was rough on her chin as he squeezed it and made her look at him. "Andrew's been patient. But he's losing his patience. Maybe I'll let him pay you a visit next time. Convince you of how much you want him."

He shoved her face away. Piper grabbed the seat of her chair to keep herself from falling over as Barret stepped through her front door without another word.

She did not want Andrew to show up there. She hated him. She knew exactly what would happen if she was left alone with that jerk. He'd do as he'd always done; try to pressure her to bed, try to bully her into pairing with him.

Piper really didn't want a mate. But if she was forced to be paired with someone, she'd rather it be her true mate, someone she could love and be friends with. Someone she actually wanted to see every single day.

Like Luke.

Nope. She had to get him out of her head. She'd run him off. And he was probably mad at her now. He probably thought she was ungrateful for his help.

But really, her concern for his presence near her home was twofold: While she hadn't lied about his presence making things worse for her, she was also worried for his own safety. She knew Barret couldn't take him alone, but it wasn't below her brother to bring as many males as he needed to hurt Luke. She couldn't handle anyone getting hurt because of her.

Piper wasn't sure how long she sat there staring at the beige carpet after Barret left. Five minutes? Ten? Sixty? It could've been hours. She couldn't make herself move. Fear had her behind cemented to the chair. She wanted to get ready for bed. She wanted to curl up with the new book she'd brought home from work. She wanted a lot of things.

Including freedom. Freedom from the cage her family was forcing her into.

Would it be so bad to be mated to Andrew? She tried to picture herself being tied to the male, tried to picture him in her space, tried to picture herself in bed with him, naked, going through the motions so he could put a cub in her belly.

That last thought got her feet moving. Toward the bathroom. To puke.

****

Luke sat in his truck, his wrists crossed over the steering wheel, and stared at his cabin. Everything in him told him to go to Piper's, just to check on her. But three days ago, she'd told him to stay away. She didn't want him near her.

But that wasn't it. She'd said him being on her property would make things worse for her. Did that mean her prick of a brother would hurt her again? How the hell could she expect him to sit on his ass and do nothing when he knew he could keep her safe. Even if he had to sleep in her woods or even on her front porch every night for the rest of his natural born life.

Starting hard when his passenger door opened, he wiped the scowl from his face and tried to soften his expression when he realized Shawnee had climbed into his truck.

"Shouldn't you be in bed?" he asked, still staring straight ahead.

"I was. I got thirsty. What are you doing out here?" she asked. He could see her looking at him from his periphery, but didn't turn his head to make eye contact.

"Thinking," he said.

No matter what happened, he could never and *would* never be mean to the women in his life. Or *any* woman, for that matter. Shawnee could Shift right there and start clawing him to ribbons and he wouldn't be able to fight back. He'd sit there and take it until she wore herself out. He could never hurt a female.

"About what?" Her voice was soft and a little scratchy from sleep. It was barely after three in the morning. And he'd been in his truck for the last two hours. He was kind of surprised she was only now coming out to investigate.

Luke clenched his teeth until his jaw hurt. He'd already spilled his guts to Shawnee and Colton. Why hold back now?

"Piper."

He finally glanced at Shawnee to see her looking at his cabin, nodding slowly as if she understood everything from that one word.

"You want me to go with you?" she asked, turning to look at him again. She looked surprised his face was turned toward hers.

His nostrils flared as he inhaled deep and turned forward again, dropping his head against the seat rest. "No. But thanks."

"You really think it's worse if you're hanging around? I mean, how could it be worse if they can't touch her since you're there."

He shrugged. He didn't have that answer. He'd only been staying the nights there. Those fuckers could've paid her a visit any time in the day, but they'd stayed away. Because they could scent him? Or did they wait until she was at her most vulnerable, like when she was asleep?

"Go to bed. Get some sleep. You've got work tomorrow."

Shawnee worked at Moe's, Noah's bar, alongside Noah and his mate Hollyn. Even after she and Colton had fallen stupidly in love, she'd demanded she still work. It was a freedom she'd never had before leaving her last Pride. Or even when she was still in her family Pride. Colton would never take that away from her.

"I'm pregnant," Shawnee blurted.

That made Luke's head swing around to gawk at her. "What?"

"Colton doesn't know yet. I'm waiting to find the perfect time to tell him."

Shawnee was pregnant. And she'd told Luke first. How the hell was he supposed to keep this kind of secret? And now, he couldn't convince himself to leave the territory. He needed to stay near his Clan sister to keep her safe. She'd have at least two cubs growing in her belly, possibly more, although there was always the slim chance it would just be one bear cub instead of multiple lion cubs.

"Thanks," Luke said, turning to look at her again.

"For what?" she asked, her ruddy brows pinched in confusion.

"For trusting me with your secret."

She shrugged and a smile softened her expression. "Someday, your mate will be telling me the same thing."

And with that, she pushed the door open and stepped out. She softly pushed the door shut so she didn't wake up the rest of the Clan and headed back into her own cabin.

Of course she'd get that last jab in. She didn't understand. He didn't want a mate. Couldn't have one. If he was this obsessed with protecting a woman he barely knew, how bad would it be if he actually had a woman he loved? He'd be crazier than Micah from Big River.

Luke leaned forward and dropped his head against the wheel. He'd thought hearing that he'd be an uncle would've killed the urge to leave the territory. Instead, he found the need to check on Piper even stronger. What the fuck did that say about him that he was willing to leave his fragile sister to keep a stranger safe?

It said his need to protect was just as strong as it had been all those years ago.

And with that thought came the sounds of his childhood and teen years. The screams. The tears. The curses. The breaking glass.

"Fuck," he muttered under his breath.

He couldn't fight it. Either he made sure Piper was okay or he'd end up having to Shift again. If his mind was torn the way it was, if his mind was as poisoned with memories as it was at that moment, his bear would be volatile and dangerous. He couldn't risk that.

Starting his truck with a wince and a prayer that no one woke to the rumbling, he backed out of the driveway and headed toward Dittmer. At least she was fairly close to Blackwater territory.

When he was close enough, he pulled onto the same piece of road he always did, jogged into the woods, pulled his clothes off and Shifted. He didn't bother tying his clothes to his leg; he didn't plan on seeing her again tonight. She was probably sound asleep. The whole town seemed to be. Except him. Except Luke. He never seemed to sleep anymore.

Every light in her house was dark. He couldn't hear any sounds coming from inside indicating she was still awake. But there were new scents around her property. Similar to hers, but different enough to know she'd had a visitor. Similar – her brother maybe? Had that piece of shit come knocking on her door the second Luke wasn't around?

He cursed in his head as his bear thought about hunting down the brother and scaring him enough to stay away from Piper permanently. Instead, Luke walked further into the yard, taking long, silent strides as he moved closer and closer, and then, he did something he'd never admit to another living soul – he allowed his bear to piss in Piper's yard.

Luke's scent, his bear's scent, would cover her property well enough to deter anyone from coming around, at least until it rained. It would smell like he'd been there recently and on a regular basis.

Smiling inwardly, Luke watched as bear carried them away from her house, through the woods, and gave Luke his skin back before they were too close to the road. And now, he was smiling outwardly. Fuck her brother. Fuck her family if they thought he'd just roll over and let them bully and beat her.

Luke grabbed his clothes from the ground and only bothered tugging on his jeans and shirt and drove home barefoot. As he neared Blackwater territory, his smile began to fade. What if he'd, once again, made things worse for her. She'd said him being there would make things worse. Now, her property was covered with his scent. There'd be no doubt to any Shifter who wandered close enough that he'd been there. What would happen to her now? Had he just condemned her to more mistreatment?

Luke slammed his hand against the steering wheel. He turned his eyes toward the dark sky and prayed for rain to wash away his stupidity. Why the fuck had he done that? It almost felt like he'd been claiming her. But she wasn't his to claim. And he didn't want a fucking mate. He would never be like his dad.

The sun would be up in a few hours, but at least it was the weekend; he could sleep in for a while. And he needed it. He'd been running on fumes for far too long. His people needed him sharp and strong, especially now that Shawnee was pregnant. Luke knew Colton was fully capable of taking care of and protecting his own mate. That didn't mean that incessant need to protect those he cared about wasn't going to push every other rational thought aside and cause him to sleep on their porch like he'd done when Hollyn had come into Blackwater.

He was dragging ass as he parked his truck and shuffled into his cabin. He'd left his shoes in his truck but hadn't even noticed the gravel biting into the soles of his feet with every step. His body was numb and shaky from exhaustion. He needed sleep. He needed to protect Piper. He needed to protect Shawnee. He needed for all the memories to die a painful death and give him peace for once in his life.

Dropping onto his bed with an *oomph*, he turned his head to the side and closed his eyes. He didn't pull off his clothes and climb under the blankets. He didn't have the energy for even something that small.

Within seconds, he was falling into those weird in between dreams where he wasn't quite asleep and wasn't quite awake. And for some reason, every single time he tried to push his mind in a different direction, Piper's pretty green eyes filled the scene in every single dream.

Chapter Three

Luke sat at the table with his Clan brothers and one of their mates, June. She was Carter's mate and new to the Clan. Luke liked her. She was witty and didn't take crap from anyone. She was also almost twice the size of most the women he knew so he didn't feel the constant need to protect her. Well that, and Carter was so freaking crazy about her he barely let her out of his sight except for when one of them had to go to work. And since June still worked in a place crowded with humans, only Carter and sometimes Shawnee would visit her there.

Luke was unstable and feared he'd screw shit up for Shifters if he hung out at her job with their stand-in Alpha. He'd only gone once and that had almost turned into a disaster.

He'd slept until almost noon that afternoon and, honestly, probably could've slept longer. But Carter and June beat on his door, telling him it was time to get up. In other words, they wanted to hang out at Moe's for a while and were doing their best to get him out of his cabin. Had Colton and Shawnee told Carter what was going on? Or were they like everyone else and picked up on his permanent funky mood? He trusted any of his brothers to keep his secret, but that didn't mean he was ready to tell anyone else yet. Especially after last night. What the fuck had he been thinking?

Shawnee set a bucket of beer on the table and held her pen over the order pad. "You guys going to eat?"

Carter, June, and Colton ordered, but Luke shook his head and forced a closed-lipped smile at her. She knew what was going on, knew why his mood had been sour as fuck lately. She shot him a sad smile and patted his shoulder as she passed, squeezing it once to comfort him.

Didn't work.

Why the fuck was he so obsessed over this one woman? Yeah. He wanted to keep her safe. He wanted to keep every woman in the world safe, but he knew that was literally impossible. And he had his own people to protect, especially Shawnee. Fuck. When was she going to tell Colton and everyone else? He kind of hated being the only one in the know. All it would take is one slip of a single word and he'd blow her secret all to hell.

His brain was fried. He couldn't focus on one damn thought. Round and round they went, until he felt dizzy.

Dropping his head into his hands, he listened to the conversation going on around him and tried to focus in on the conversation, tried to focus on anything.

"You okay?" June asked from beside him, her hand soft on his forearm as he propped his elbows on the table top and massaged his temples.

Luke dropped his hands and crossed them over his forearms. "Yeah. I'm good," he lied. He didn't even bother trying to smile at June. She'd see right through him.

As he watched his friends interact and groaned when a few members of Big River stepped through the door, Luke fought with his bear. He wanted out again. He wanted to run again. He wanted to check on Piper again.

Not now. Sun's up, he told his bear, trying to barter with him.

But his bear remained restless in his head. And then Luke realized he'd been relatively quiet up until the last few minutes.

The door to Moe's opened and a slice of sun cut across the floor, interrupted by a thin shadow. A scent hit his nose and he instantly knew why his bear was so agitated: Piper.

What the hell was she doing at Moe's? He didn't remember ever seeing her in there before, not that he would've noticed her before that night in the parking lot. He would've just seen another woman in the place, another thin, pretty female in the bar.

Bull shit.

Luke started at his bear's words. Since when did his animal argue with him?

Her eyes were narrowed as she stood just inside the door and looked around the room. And then she zeroed in on him and crossed the room, anger all over her pretty face. Her pretty swollen face. Wait…what?

"Were you at my house last night?" she asked when she was close enough. She wasn't at work, yet she was still wearing a blouse, a sweater, and slacks. Even her shoes were all fancy and prim. Her hair was smooth, silky and straight as it barely grazed her shoulders, and her green eyes were full of fire. One of them looked swollen, too, but he couldn't detect any bruising. Maybe she was just tired.

"What?" he asked, trying to focus on what the hell she was saying instead of how she looked. Why the hell should he care whether she wanted to dress like a librarian on her days off?

"Were you at my house last night, Luke?" she asked, crossing her arms over her chest and leaning her weight on one foot, making one of her thin hips pop to the side.

Of course she would've smelled him all over her property. The point had been to deter others, not piss her off.

Instead of lying, he nodded once. "Yeah."

"When?"

Luke looked around at his friends watching him closely, their faces a mixture of confusion and curiosity.

Pushing to his feet, Luke waved his hand toward the door. No way was he having this conversation in front of everyone. He hated that he'd had a moment of weakness and admitted everything to Colton and Shawnee. If everyone else found out, he wouldn't hear the end of it, especially from Reed. That asshole would probably call Nova and she'd rush over to get all the details and stick her nose in his business.

But when Luke stood, Piper tensed and took a step back, jerking her head back and flinching away in fear. What the fuck? He hadn't made any quick moves, hadn't raised either of his hands, hadn't raised his voice.

And then he got a closer look at her face. She was wearing a lot of makeup, more than he'd seen her wear yet, although he'd only really been close to her the one night she'd taken him shopping with her. Not only was her face puffy and swollen in places, but he could see light bruising beneath that makeup.

Her fucking brother had hit her again.

Giving Piper a wide berth, he moved toward the door, only glancing back once to make sure she was following him, and stepped outside. He held the door for her, then jerked his chin for her to follow him to his truck. After she climbed into his passenger seat, he rounded the truck and got in the driver's seat.

"Where are we going?" she asked, her voice a lot smaller than it had been just moments ago. And he could smell the fear rolling from her. She was afraid of Luke now? He'd given her no reason to fear him nor would he ever.

"Nowhere. I just wanted to talk," Luke said, keeping his body faced forward and his hands on the steering wheel so she could see them. He knew what she was going through. He might not have given her a reason to fear him, but she was still suffering the after effects of abuse. It wasn't something that went away overnight. Or ever.

"Why were you there? I asked you to stop coming over."

"Truth?" he said, turning his head just enough to look at her.

"Of course," she said, her body pressed against the door, keeping as much space as she could between them.

"I needed to know you were safe."

She inhaled deeply and released a long sigh. Her eyes closed, blocking him from seeing their pretty color, and she nodded. "That's what I figured. You didn't have to…pee in my yard, though." Her cheeks flushed pink at the word *pee*. What would she think if she knew he had a pretty bad habit of cussing? Would those pretty cheeks flush even deeper?

Fuck. He had to stop seeing her as pretty. He couldn't let himself think that way.

"Do you know about my Pride?"

His brows dropped as he waited for her to finish. Luke shook his head and waited for her to finish.

"I'm a cougar. From the Donnell Pride. My dad is the Alpha."

He'd heard of the Donnell Pride, but didn't know much about them. The fact the daughter of an Alpha was being treated so fucking badly was a little surprising. Although, the daughter of an Alpha would be a hot commodity to any male wanting to climb the ranks in his Pride. Sometimes, Luke was glad as fuck he'd been born a bear and didn't have to deal with those kinds of politics. He'd just had other shit to deal with growing up.

She waited for him to react. He wasn't sure what the fuck he was supposed to react to – the fact she was from Donnell or the fact she was an Alpha's daughter.

"You don't know about Donnell Pride, do you?"

"Just that you're from west of Festus."

"We *were* from west of Festus. My dad moved us closer to St. Louis County a few years ago. Said he wanted more opportunity to add to our numbers."

"Power hungry," Luke guessed.

She nodded slowly. "Something like that. Dad didn't even care what kind of Shifter he recruited, as long as they were feline. And he was pissed that he only got one daughter out of eight of us. That's less chance of popping out a bunch of cubs."

So her dad was one of those kinds of fuckers. He hated those pieces of shit, the kind of males who thought their daughters were nothing more than ovaries and a uterus.

"The laws changed. He can't force you to do anything," Luke said, taking deep breaths to stay calm. She didn't even have to say anything else; he knew exactly where this conversation was going.

"But they can bully me until I give in," she said so softly he'd almost missed it. She looked so sad and defeated. The bruises on her face were more obvious in the sunlight, no matter how hard she tried to cover them with makeup.

Luke's eyes roamed her face, taking in every single inch of damage that fucker had done to her. Waving his hand in her direction, he bit back the growl that tried to work up his throat. "Your brother do that?"

She inhaled and sighed again, but didn't answer. She didn't need to. That had been the scent he'd picked up last night. Similar to Piper's but different.

"Because I was there last night?"

Piper shook her head this time. "No. This is a few days old."

That confused him as he frowned at her. "How is it a few days old? Your Shifter healing should've…" And then it hit him. She was healing. Which meant the damage was way worse than what he was seeing. He'd beat her so badly it'd taken days just to get to this point.

Yet, she was right there, talking to him, holding her head up, even if she was terrified of the world around her.

"I can help," he said, unable to hold back the growl this time. And then he wanted to punch himself in the dick when she pressed herself even closer to the door at that sound. *You're scaring her*, he told his bear as he continued to thrash around inside Luke's head. He was pissed. Someone had hurt Piper and he wanted blood.

"How? Just being around me is dangerous."

She was chewing on her bottom lip now as her hands remained folded in her lap. She looked like she was in church or something the way she sat so primly, her back ramrod straight.

Dangerous. How was it dangerous? "Dangerous for who?"

She turned her head toward him and stopped worrying her lip. "Both of us. If you keep coming around, the punishments will get worse. He's already threatened to let Andrew come to my house."

"Who's Andrew?"

"And if they catch you there…Barrett can't beat you. He knows that. So he'll bring other guys from the Pride to hurt you. It's just a matter of time."

She went to push from the truck and he did the stupidest thing he'd ever done and reached out, grabbed her arm, and kept her from leaving.

She tensed and threw one hand up in front of her face.

Luke didn't release her arm, didn't say anything, just waited for her to realize he wasn't a threat. When her arms relaxed the tiniest amount, he loosened his grip, but he still didn't release her. He had more questions. And he didn't want to chase her to her car. That would freak her out all that much more.

"Piper," he said, keeping his voice soft and steady. "Look at me."

It took her a few seconds, but she eventually turned her pretty face toward him. He'd noticed freckles across her nose and cheeks that night at the grocery store. But they were covered with makeup. Pity. They made her look young, sweet, endearing.

"I'm not afraid of your fucking brother or Pride. I can protect you. Let me help you. Please," he begged. He couldn't fail her. He couldn't fail yet another female. It'd kill him.

Piper carefully pulled her arm from his grasp, but she didn't climb out of his truck. In fact, she reached out and pulled the door shut, as if she was afraid someone would see her sitting there with him. She probably was. If him simply being on her property was causing her so many problems, what would happen to her if she was caught hanging out with him.

"Who's Andrew?"

Her light brows pulled together, causing a tiny crease between them. "What?"

"You said he threatened to let Andrew come over. Who is he?"

She was no longer sitting up straight. She hunched forward a little and brushed imaginary lint off her pants. "My mate. Er, well, the guy my parents want me to pair up with. I don't want him. I don't want a mate. And if I did, I want to pick my own guy. I want a normal life where I decide whether or not I have kids. And he's a slob. And mean. And..." She trailed off with a shake of her head. "It doesn't matter."

"Which part?"

"All of it."

"Yeah, it does. You have the right to want your own life," he said. If any of his friends heard him holding a full conversation with another living soul, they'd have a damn stroke.

But talking to her felt different. He didn't feel the need to close her off or hide shit from her. He had a feeling she'd be one of the only people in his life who would fully understand his need to protect those he loved. And even those he barely knew. Like her.

Her thin shoulders shrugged up. She was pretty skinny. And her chest was kind of flat. But the tiny tits she did have were perky and fit her body shape perfectly.

What...the...fuck? Why was he constantly checking her out and obsessing over her face and body? He must be losing his fucking mind.

****

Let me help you.

Luke's words clanged around inside Piper's head. If only it were that easy. Seriously. She'd set him up a tent right in front of her house if his mere presence would keep her safe. But he couldn't be with her every minute of every day. Eventually, her parents would get tired of her rebellion and would catch her at work. No way was she willing to risk losing her job. It was her dream job, the best part of her week. She'd grown to hate the weekends because that meant always looking over her shoulder. And no books.

"I should go," she said.

His eyes jerked to her face and it was only then that she'd noticed he'd been looking at her chest. While she should've been offended, she was instead intrigued. And...a little turned on. Luke wasn't someone she'd have normally chosen out of a crowd. But something about him made her want to tousle her hair, pull on a pair of ripped jeans, and pretend she was *Sandra Dee* at the end of *Grease*.

She chuckled at the thought, then covered it with a cough so Luke wouldn't think she was laughing at him.

"I have friends. A lot of them," he said.

Her brows pulled up and together. "Congratulations?" She didn't think he was bragging, but his words made her feel lonely. Even more so than usual.

"No," he said, shaking his head. He pulled off his ball cap, pushed a hand through his messy blonde hair, then pulled it back on. "I mean, there are a lot of us who can keep you safe."

"I have to work," she said.

"Right now?" He looked confused as his eyes roamed her body and then he nodded as if her attire made sense.

Great. Her next words were going to confirm to him that she was an oddball. "No. Not today. I mean, there's no way you can keep me safe every minute. I have a job. You have a job. Eventually, there will be a time no one will be around. It's just easier if I handle this on my own."

His eyes scanned her face, no doubt taking inventory of the healing bruises and swelling. She'd covered it all the best she could, but there was only so much drug store makeup could do for that kind of damage. She'd told her coworkers she'd tripped up her stairs and fell on her face. One of the ladies didn't look like she'd believed Piper, but she didn't say anything else.

"I can't," he said, his voice so deep and growly and manly. It did something funny to her body. Something she wasn't willing to think about or analyze.

She had no doubt Luke was a good man, or that he could keep her safe and could take care of himself. She had no doubt his people were good and would do what they could to keep her safe. But there were too many *what ifs*. What if Barrett *did* bring several males from Donnell? What if he or someone from her Pride *did* come to the library while she was at work? What if someone from his Clan was hurt because of her?

What if she fell for this broody, dark, gruff man?

"You can't what?" she asked, her eyes betraying her and dropping to his lips for the briefest second. Was he closer? He seemed closer. Like he'd leaned closer to her. Or maybe she'd leaned closer to him. She wasn't sure, but he was definitely closer now and she could see the way his whiskey colored eyes looked like honey in the sunlight.

When her eyes raised back to his face, his were glowing. The bright amber was beautiful and mesmerizing and terrifying.

"I can't…stay away."

He leaned closer and his tongue darted out to moisten his bottom lip. And then she leaned closer. It was like she had no control over her own darn mind or body anymore.

"Why?" she whispered.

Luke closed the space between them and pressed his lips to hers. A pained moaned vibrated against her lips. They didn't touch anywhere else, didn't throw their arms around each other, didn't push against each other. Just stayed like that, their lips touching, breathing each other in.

And then Luke pulled back. His eyes were squeezed shut and his brows were so furrowed she wondered if she'd done something wrong.

"I'm sorry," he said, a whole lot more growl to his voice than there had been before. He finally opened his eyes and looked at her. "I'll keep you safe. I promise. No one will ever hurt you again."

"Why?" she whispered again. He hadn't answered her the first time and it didn't look like he'd answer her this time, either.

"Will you come back in? Meet my people?" His face was full of emotions she couldn't begin to name. She was familiar with anger, hate, disappointment. But none of those were in his eyes. She wasn't sure what he was feeling, how he was looking at her.

Except…it looked a whole lot like respect. Lust, maybe. Want. Desire.

She felt all those, too. Could he see it on her face? Could he smell what that one kiss had done to her body? Could he smell her arousal? If he could, he didn't say anything or try to act on it or push her for more.

His hand raised and his fingertips touched his lips as he waited for her answer. Did he feel those same little zaps she'd felt from their touch? It had been unlike anything she'd ever experienced. And if she were honest with herself, she wanted more. She wanted to feel his lips again. She wanted to feel his strong arms wrapped around her. She wanted to feel his big strong body against hers, keeping her safe.

Dangerous thoughts. Messy thoughts. Thoughts she couldn't entertain.

Meet his people. Barrett would smell those people on her if he came over tonight. Then again, he'd smell Luke for sure. Well, if she was going to be hurt anyway, she might as well attempt to make some new friends, even if the friendships couldn't go past tonight.

With a nod, Piper pushed her door open and just kind of dropped to the gravel below. His truck was so big, just like him. The inside was full of fast food wrappers, but it smelled like him, a mixture of earth, and fur, and whatever that spicy scent that was unique to him.

Luke waited at the hood for her, let her walk ahead of him while keeping a steadying, strong hand at her lower back. Her nerves kicked up and her stomach hurt. She wanted to turn back around and run to her car the second they stepped inside. But then what? Sit in her empty, quiet house and wonder whether Barrett or Andrew would show up?

"You're not going to tell them everything are you?" she whispered low enough no one but him would hear.

He nodded, then winked. And shoot, if it wasn't sexy. He was teasing her. He hadn't seemed like the playful type, but maybe she was wrong about him.

The table where he'd been sitting was filled with a bunch of really big guys and a couple of females. She'd have preferred to have way more women around. Men scared her, whether she wanted to admit it or not. Except Luke. He'd been the first male she'd encountered in her entire life who didn't constantly intimidate Piper.

Luke made her feel safe, at least while he was around. But the second he was gone, she went right back to constantly looking over her shoulder and anticipating and fearing the next time a family member, namely her oldest brother, Barrett, would show up.

Let me help you.

But how? Like she'd already told him, there was no way for him to watch over her twenty-four hours a day. And she wouldn't want him to do that, anyway. He had his own life, his own friends, his own people to care for. She'd just be a distraction in his life.

Luke started pointing people out and introducing them. "This is Colton and Carter from my Clan. That's June, Carter's mate. And…" He craned his neck to look around the room. "The redhead over there with the tray is Colton's mate. The two bartenders are from my Clan, too. That's Noah and Hollyn."

"Holy shit, dude. He's talking," a guy whispered, but Piper had heard him.

"The smartass is Reed," Luke said, pointing to the guy who'd whispered. Reed grinned wide and waved at her and Piper couldn't help the huff of surprised laughter at his personality. He was so…silly.

"That's Emory and Eli. The blonde is Peyton and her mate Tristan. And the guy glaring at you like an asshole is Micah and the sweet girl beside him is Callie. They're all from Big River."

"Not us," the tiny woman Luke introduced as Emory said. "We're from Hope Pride."

Piper nodded. She'd heard about Hope Pride. Had even been tempted to ask them if she could stay there. That way, there'd be safety in numbers. But she also knew about the kind of women who lived in that Pride, the kind of lives they'd come from. She wouldn't subject them to any more chaos. Because she knew if she moved there, there'd definitely be chaos. No way would her parents just give up on her merely because she joined another group of Shifters.

"Pleasure to meet you all," she said, dipping her head. Luke pulled the chair out for her, so she sat, crossing her legs at the knees and folding her hands in her lap.

Emory frowned the slightest bit at her, but then that crease smoothed. "Where you from, Piper?"

"Um, originally, Donnell Pride," she said, looking up at Luke when he sat in the chair beside her. He was leaned forward, his forearms resting on the table. A quick look around and she realized everyone was slouching in their chairs, leaning against their mates, or leaning forward the way Luke was. How rigid she must look to them.

Piper attempted to sit the way Luke was, but instantly felt silly and straightened back up.

"Donnell Pride?" Carter asked, his eyes narrowed.

"You know them?" she asked. Luke wasn't touching her, but she could feel the warmth coming from him. It made her feel anchored and steady.

"*Of* them. Never actually met anyone from there. But yeah..." Now his dark brows were pulled low. He looked angry. At her? No way. She hadn't done anything to earn his anger.

But men were always angry for one reason or another. Always angry at women for one reason or another. At least in her experience.

"What brings you to our little slice of heaven?" Reed asked, popping the top of a beer and offering it to her. She crinkled her nose and shook her head. "Don't like beer?" he asked, pulling his hand back with an appalled expression. But even that look seemed silly to her, like he was doing it to get a reaction out of her.

"Not that kind," Piper said.

The redhead Luke said was Shawnee, the mate to one of his Clan brothers, showed up at their table. "What can I get you instead? If you're into cocktails, Hollyn," she said, jerking her head toward the woman tossing a bottle over her shoulder behind the bar. "Can give you a real show."

"Do you have *Heineken*?" Piper asked, then pulled her bottom lip between her teeth when she caught everyone staring at her. "Or water. Water's fine, too."

"No," Shawnee said, frowning at someone behind Piper. "We have *Heineken*. Be right back."

"Dude! You drink real beer! Not that chick stuff, but real beer," Reed said, half standing and raising his hand for a high five. Piper giggled and slapped her hand against his. "Okay. Real beer but girl high five. That's cool, though," Reed said, his eyes darting to Luke beside Piper.

Piper looked at the gruff, sexy man; he was scowling at Reed so deep she wondered if he wouldn't get permanent wrinkles.

"What's wrong?" she whispered, leaning a little into his space in hopes no one would hear them. It was hard to have secrets around so many Shifters. And she could tell the entire place was full of them.

He turned his head to look down at her and his eyes held the slightest glow. And then they dipped down to her lips for a brief second before raising again. Was he thinking about their kiss in his truck? Because she sure was now.

"I didn't want him to upset you," he said with a tiny shrug.

She frowned and smiled at the same time. He was worried his friend would upset her? With his playful comment? That was so different from what she was used to. He was so different from the men she was used to.

"He didn't upset me. I could tell he was playing," she said with a soft smile. And then her eyes dipped to his lips.

The room seemed to fall away as they sat there staring at each other, just…being with each other. She'd read about moments like this in books but had never experienced anything like it. She wasn't sure at the time she wanted to; with Luke, she really, *really* liked it.

"What's going on?" someone whispered. A female. Piper had no idea which one because she didn't really know their voices yet. But that soft sound was enough to snap Luke back to reality.

Shame. Piper would've been happy with where their little moment was going.

Wait. What the hell was going on inside her head? Kissing led to other things. Like pairing and mating and slavery.

She shouldn't have come back in. She should've gotten in her little car and headed back home. Actually, she needed to stop by the store again. She was already out of bacon. And milk. And beer. And after her kiss from Luke and then the *almost* kiss from Luke, she'd need at least a few more before she was able to sleep tonight.

If only Luke could sleep at her house. She'd feel safe. She'd *be* safe. At least physically. Her heart was a whole other matter.

Chapter Four

"Why did you want me to meet your friends?" Piper asked, fumbling with her keys beside her car.

"I wanted you to see they're good people. That blonde? Peyton? If she found out what you're going through…" He did this shiver thing and then situated his ball cap on his head.

"What? What would she do?" What could she do? She wasn't all that much bigger than Piper. It was obvious she was a Shifter, too, and Luke had said she was with Big River Pack which made her a wolf.

"Peyton's animal was forced on her. Her wolf is…well, one of my friends, Nova, calls her animal *Cujo*."

"Like that movie from the eighties?" Piper asked, pushing the button on her fob to unlock the door.

"Yeah. Her wolf kept attacking members of Big River. They figured out it was because her wolf thought they were a threat…to Callie."

Piper ran the faces through her mind. There had only been three women sitting with them. Callie was the smaller blonde, the one with the guy who'd glared at her all night. Luke had made a few comments, but Emory said to ignore Micah. She'd tried, but it was hard. Luke sitting beside her made her feel safe. And if he was a friend of Luke's, she knew he wouldn't hurt her. There was no way someone like Luke would socialize or befriend a jerk.

"Callie's her friend?"

"Well, not at first. I mean, she didn't know Callie before she met and mated with Tristan. But Callie…" He inhaled through his nose, causing his nostrils to flare. "She was supposed to be mated to a dickhead. She ran and ended up at Big River. Peyton's wolf saw Callie as vulnerable, weak, and wanted to protect her."

"I assume you have a point to make," Piper said, crossing her arms over her chest. Did that mean Peyton or her wolf thought Piper was a threat to Callie or her friends?

"Peyton is going to be on winter break soon for the holidays. She could hang out at the library with you during the day. And so can Callie and even Emory on her days off. I can be there at night. We can keep you safe."

His eyes had that glow again, even as he held his hand up to shield them from the sun. They were like the sun itself, the light whiskey color fading with his wolf's amber glow.

"Luke—"

"Let me help. Please. I can't…" His sentence trailed off.

"Can't what?"

He dropped his hand to his side and balled it into a fist. "I can't fail you. I can't fail again."

Piper's brows drew together. What did that mean? How could he fail her again when they'd barely known each other longer than a few months? Technically, it was only about a week or so since they'd only officially met the first time when she'd called him out of the trees lining her yard.

Piper pulled her bottom lip into her mouth and chewed it as she watched a thousand emotions fly across Luke's face. If she agreed to this, there were so many possible outcomes. She could still end up falling prey to her family or Pride. Luke or his friends could get hurt. Or…

Or she could finally get the freedom she'd always dreamed of. Maybe even make some new friends. A lot of new friends.

Luke's eyes were on her mouth again and her tongue darted out to moisten them. It was a mystery to her why her lips felt so dry every time they earned Luke's attention.

And then he closed the space between them and crashed his lips down on hers. His hand cupped the back of her head and she moaned. Gripping his shirt in two fists, she stepped closer until their bodies were touching, her head tilted back, her chest heaving against his.

Just like in the truck, he didn't try to push his tongue into her mouth, didn't try to deepen the kiss or push for anything more than his lips against hers.

When Luke finally pulled back with one of those sexy smacks of his lips, he kept his hand on the back of her head and leaned his forehead against hers, his breath warming her face as he panted. They were both out of breath and hadn't done anything more than a simple kiss.

"Okay," she breathed out before her brain had a chance to catch up to her mouth.

Luke jerked back, his hand still cupping her head, and looked at her with brows up to his hairline.

"Okay? You'll let me help you? You'll let me keep you safe?"

Piper laid her hands on Luke's chest and urged him back a step. She was getting far too comfortable being near him. And she was getting to like his kisses way too much and craving more from him.

"One condition," she said.

"Name it," he said, surprise and relief still on his face.

"If it gets too dangerous for anyone, especially you, the deal's off."

His brows dropped to a frown so fast his ears moved. "How the hell would it get dangerous for me?"

"My Pride isn't exactly honorable, Luke. The second they find out what's going on, they'll move on to plan B. Then C. And D. And so on. Barrett will bring every single one of his buddies if he thinks he can't beat you in a fight."

"He can't," Luke said. He wasn't being cocky. He was confident in his fighting abilities and his bear.

She'd also seen how strong he was and how fast his fists could move back at the grocery store parking lot.

"Which means he'll definitely bring a group of people to attack you. I can't be the cause of any injury or pain to you or any of your friends. I'm scared my parents will send more people to the library. Do you really believe Callie or Peyton could take multiple Shifters on at once?"

"Peyton can," he said without missing a bit.

"But not Callie."

"We all work and live nearby. If you even think there's a risk you call or text me immediately. I'll bring a fucking army with me."

"An army of Shifters," she said and giggled. He was being serious, she could tell, but now she was picturing all those people inside in camouflage.

"Something like that," he said, a tiny smile on his lips. "Sorry about kissing you again. Don't know why I keep doing that." He pulled his hat off and pushed his hand through his hair the way he'd done in his truck.

"It's okay," she said, ducking her gaze and lowering her head to hide the heat that rushed her cheeks. She wasn't sure whether she'd said that as an acceptance of his apology or because she'd liked it. Or both.

Luke's finger lifted her chin until she had to look at him. "Will you be okay until I get there tonight?"

Her brows pulled together in confusion. Did he really think she needed to be around him all the time? Wait. That's not what he was asking. He wasn't like Andrew. He didn't think all women should worship the ground he walked on. He was simply asking if she'd be safe until he arrived on her property tonight.

Did he think he had to sleep in the woods like he had the first few weeks? And did she have the courage to invite him inside over night? He could always take the guest room. She'd had it set up since she'd moved into her house. Not because she thought she'd have company, but because she didn't know what else to do with that room and leaving it empty felt wrong to her.

"I'll be fine," she said, fully aware her voice wavered enough for Luke to know she was bluffing.

"You want me to follow you home?" His eyes bounced between hers, their whiskey color hypnotizing her until she was willing to agree to just about anything he asked.

That thought snapped her back to reality. She was getting too comfortable around him. Not just for safety, but more like she wanted him in her life every day. Too dangerous. More dangerous than her brother. Because while bruises and cuts healed, emotional scars were permanent.

Piper stepped back until her body was pressed against her car. Luke's eyes narrowed, but he took a step away, too, giving her space.

"I'll be fine," she repeated with a nod. She didn't smile and was having a hard time making eye contact. She was trying her hardest to shut down her emotions and feared her eyes would give her away.

When Luke was far enough back for her to open the door, she slid in her seat and pulled the door shut quickly. She didn't look up at Luke as she backed out of her space, didn't look in the mirror as she pulled out of the parking lot. But she knew he was still standing there, still watching her. As if she could feel those whiskey colored eyes on her, even long after she was out of his line of sight.

The second Piper stepped into her house, she toed off her shoes and carried them to the closet. Then she pulled off her clothes, slipped on her work clothes which consisted of a pair of jeans and a t-shirt, then got to work scrubbing the house from top to bottom. She wasn't positive she'd invite Luke into her house tonight, but just in case, she wanted to make sure it was clean.

As she scrubbed her ball and claw tub, she ran the day through her mind. His friends had been so warm and welcoming and fun. They'd teased each other and included her in the conversation whenever they could. She'd still felt out of place, but that hadn't been their fault. She always felt out of place, always felt like a square peg trying to squeeze into a circle hole.

His friends looked relaxed. They were happy. And she'd sat there like a statue, her posture perfect as always. Her clothes were total opposite of theirs. The women's hair was even…relaxed. If that was even possible. Ponytails and soft waves instead of the way her hair had been flat ironed straight and sprayed into submission.

Piper tossed her rag into the washing machine and pulled her rubber gloves off and looked around the house. It was already clean. Why was she scrubbing it even more?

Stupid question: This house, the way she kept it, the way she dressed, the way she lived, they were the only things she had any control over. Luke would never understand. He'd just think she was weird, wonder why the hell he'd kissed someone with so many issues.

Why had he kissed her? Why hadn't she stopped him? They'd both agreed they didn't want mates. So why had that kiss felt so normal, so natural, so…perfect.

****

Luke sat at the table with his friends and listened as they made plans to keep Piper safe while he was at work. He couldn't help the ghost of a smile that quirked the corners of his lips up at their strategies.

"You should've told us earlier," Micah said, his eyes bright as he glared at Luke. He was always glaring at someone, including Piper. But Luke got it. After all the crap the Pack had gone through over the past couple of years, the dude was leery of anyone new. He treated everyone as a threat.

"It wasn't my story to tell," Luke said as he lifted his beer bottle to his lips.

"We could've kept her safe this whole time," Peyton said.

Luke nodded but didn't say anything else.

"We'll take care of her, brother," Colton said with a hard clap on Luke's back.

"I know," Luke said.

And he did. He knew his people would take care of Piper because Luke had asked. That's all it took. Maybe Micah was right; Luke should've told everyone sooner. Then maybe Piper could've avoided her current bruises.

Luke glanced at Colton as Shawnee passed. She caught him looking, narrowed her eyes, and shook her head the slightest bit. She still hadn't told him. When Colton found out he was going to be a dad would he still be so gung-ho about keeping Piper safe? Everyone knew how hard it was on a feline Shifter to be pregnant. Because they tended to have multiples, they ended up having to slow down and, most times, go on bed rest for a majority of their pregnancy. Shawnee was going to have a hard time with that part. She already hated to take a single day off work; she'd be miserable when she couldn't work for a couple of months.

But Luke knew the Clan and wolf Pack would keep her company. Until that point, Luke had to focus his attention on Piper.

He knew he could keep Piper safe, but there had to be more to their plan. He had to find a way to get her Pride off her back permanently. Because, eventually, he'd have to focus his attention on his Clan sister.

But what if…

What if Piper was in his life permanently? What if he did like the rest of his Clan and built a life with her?

What the fuck was he even thinking? He didn't want a mate. No matter how much his bear begged him to be near Piper or how wonderful and soft her lips felt.

He hadn't meant to kiss her. Twice. His body had just reacted. One minute they'd been talking and the next his lips were pressed against hers.

That little sound she'd made the second time caused his dick to twitch in his jeans. He had to remember what he was doing, why he was around her in the first place. And it had nothing to do with getting in her pants.

Piper wasn't even his type. Although, he wasn't really sure what his type was. She was skinny, had small tits, and was so prim and proper. Even after sitting with his people for two hours, she'd never relaxed into her chair, just sat there, watching everyone, smiling politely when appropriate, her hands folded in her lap and her legs crossed at the knees.

He was her complete opposite. Shit. Every single person he knew was her complete opposite. Except maybe Shawnee in the beginning.

Was that why she behaved and dressed the way she did? Did she think she was supposed to behave a certain way? Hopefully, after spending more time with the women of Blackwater and Big River, she'd find her own style, find herself and learn to let go a little.

But what if she didn't? Could he spend his life with someone who wore fucking cardigans every day?

Mother fucker. He was once again thinking about her as a permanent fixture in his life. How the fuck was he supposed to keep his emotional distance and see her as another woman who needed his fists when he couldn't stop picturing her by his side?

Maybe him staying on her property every night was a bad idea. He could always ask one of the other men in his Clan or even Big River to take a turn. Who was he fooling? Every single member of both his Clan and the Pack were paired up and mated. And the panthers from Ravenwood were in another state. He wouldn't bother them unless it was an emergency. They had their own battles to deal with; they didn't need the bull shit of an antiquated Pride on top of it.

It had to be Luke. And he had to get his shit together, his mind in the game and off of Piper's soft lips. And fuck, they'd been soft as hell.

He still wasn't sure why he'd kissed her. And why the fuck she didn't stop him or push him away. Instead, she'd wrapped her small hands in his shirt and clung to him for life.

Dangerous. Too fucking dangerous. All of it. And not to him physically. To both of them emotionally. He wasn't mate material. He refused to risk it. He refused to risk becoming his dad.

Once the plans were set as to who would be where with Piper, Luke said his thanks and goodbyes, accepting a hug from Shawnee as he neared the door.

Luke leaned down until his lips were near her ear and whispered as softly as he could, "You need to tell him soon."

A soft growl was his only answer as he winked down at the little redhead and headed out the door. He had somewhere to be. Piper was alone and the sun would be down soon.

If he was lucky, her brother or some other jackass from her Pride would be there and he could work out a little of his frustration at himself on their face. That thought brought a smile to his face as he aimed his truck toward her property.

He passed the place where he usually parked his truck for the night and drove right up her driveway, parked beside her little Toyota Camry, and killed the engine. Her curtains parted and she was standing there, a hand raised awkwardly at him. Luke nodded back, then pushed from the truck and tried to decide where he'd stay for the night.

He could hang out in his truck or on the porch, or he could Shift and prowl through the woods and let his bear have his body for a few hours before dawn.

Any plans he might have had changed the second the front door with the floral wreath opened and Piper stepped onto the porch.

"Hey," she said. She was no longer wearing the slacks and cardigan. She'd changed into a pair of worn in jeans and a soft looking t-shirt that hugged her body instead of hiding it.

He'd been wrong; she wasn't skinny and shapeless. Well, she was still thin and was barely a B cup, but she had a tiny waist that made her hips round out. She had a nice body. So why did she always hide it behind those baggy sweaters?

She also smelled like cleaning products. The scent overpowered her natural scent and made his bear uneasy. Her natural scent was a mixture of something citrusy, like lemons and sunshine. It was clean and fresh and sweet.

Fuuuuck. *Stop thinking about the way she smells, asshole.*

"Hey," he finally answered after staring at her like a dumbass. "You okay? Anyone stop by before I got here?"

Her head shook side to side, making her hair graze across her shoulders. "No. It would've been a couple more days, anyway," she said with a shrug.

"I hate how fucking blasé you are about that," he blurted out before he had time to put his filter in place.

She winced and wrinkled her nose. "It's my reality. My normal. Should I be shaking and crying instead?"

Luke narrowed his eyes at Piper. She was a strong one, he'd give her that. She was willing to endure beating after beating to have her own life, to have freedom from that Andrew douche. Luke couldn't wait to meet Andrew. And Barrett. He definitely couldn't wait to see Barrett again. He'd deliver twice the damage to that fucker's face that Barret had done to Piper's.

Were there more? Were there bruises under her clothes that he couldn't see? Or were they all healed up? And why the fuck did her brother insist on leaving so many fucking marks? This Andrew prick must really be a dumbass if he didn't care if his future mate was battered and bruised. Or maybe he was like Barrett and thought a woman deserved it if she went against him.

Memories. Too many fucking memories. Luke had to shut that shit down now so he could focus on Piper, on keeping her safe.

"You want to come in?" Piper asked, her brows still pinched together.

Luke looked from Piper to her front door and back. Cleaning products. She'd been cleaning because he was coming over. He didn't want to go inside, didn't want to get too comfortable with her or her fucking scent. But if the inside smelled the way she currently did, at least he wouldn't be covered when he left her place.

"Yeah. Sure," he said and resisted the urge to shuffle his feet. This felt dangerously close to date stuff. He didn't do date stuff. He didn't date. Period. That shit led to worse things, like love and mating.

Piper's lips pulled up as her brows smoothed. She led the way inside and Luke bit back the groan as her ass swayed up the stairs. Why, after all these years, did this woman have his attention like this? It was like he was losing his mind and his body had gone on autopilot or some shit.

The inside of her house smelled like whatever she'd used to clean and her. And was as feminine and frilly as she was. The couch was floral, the coffee table was this white color but looked like it was old or something because there were spots of paint a little thinner than other areas. The carpet was pale, the curtains were lacey and see through, and there were house plants everywhere.

He was scared to move from the tile in front of the door.

Piper glanced back at him, then did a double take. "Come in," she said, those brows pinching together again.

Luke looked down at his shoes. Then at her feet. She was barefoot. Well, shit. He wasn't going to track dirt or mud or whatever all over her perfect carpet. He kept his floors hardwood so when he vacuumed once a month or so it was easier to clean up. Carpeting trapped everything, including his bear's hair during the winter when work was slow and he Shifted indoors and slumbered for a whole day at a time.

Crouching down to one knee, Luke untied his boots and slipped them off, leaving them right there on the tile where they couldn't dirty up Piper's pretty space.

This place fit her, though. It was dainty and soft like her. Yet, there were strong, heavy pieces, too. Just like Piper – soft and strong.

"I like your house," he said when he couldn't think of anything else to say. It was obvious she was waiting for him to start the conversation or maybe she was wondering if he was judging her. He didn't know. And he had to make sure he didn't delve too far into her emotions.

"Thanks," she said, a genuine, wide smile stretching across her face.

That was the first time he'd seen her fully lit up with joy. She was pleased that Luke liked her house. His own face split in a grin. He couldn't help himself; hers was so fucking contagious.

"It took me forever to get it to look the way I wanted," she said, looking around as if seeing it for the first time or like she was looking at it through Luke's eyes.

Luke looked around again and realized how spotless and organized it was. But that wasn't the part she was talking about. She was talking about the pristine paint job, the nicely arranged furniture, the way all the patterns seemed to work together to make it feel homey and cozy. Even if it did smell like bleach.

That smell would eventually fade, though. And the warm feeling she'd created in her home would remain. As would her personal scent.

Glimpses of his cabin flashed through his mind. His place would drive her nuts. It was chaotiv, although it didn't bother him in the least. He knew where everything was, knew where to find everything he needed.

"Are you hungry?" she asked, turning toward the kitchen, ready to start cooking if he said yes.

"I'm good. Ate at Moe's," he said, his eyes on her.

Now she didn't seem to know what to do with herself. And he wasn't sure what to say to put her at ease. Fighting. That he knew. Making women feel happy was way outside his wheelhouse.

He needed to go outside. He was getting antsy. And something else. Something he wasn't willing to admit to himself or any other fucking person.

"I'm going to…" He let the sentence trail off and bit back the groan at the look of disappointment as he stepped toward the door.

Luke didn't bother slipping his shoes back on since he planned to Shift. His senses were way stronger in his bear's form. He wanted to be able to detect anyone from Piper's Pride before they were too close. As much as he hated to admit it, there might be a situation where he'd need his Clan. He'd rather take his chances at fighting a group of them, but he was there for Piper. And if he couldn't contain the risk, someone could get past him to hurt her.

Not fucking happening.

Scooping his boots from their spot on the floor, Luke headed onto the porch, setting his shoes down and tugging his shirt over his head as he climbed down the stairs. He'd wait until he was in the tree line before he shoved his pants down to his ankles. No way would he flash Piper a glimpse of his junk. For some reason, the thought of those pretty green eyes ogling his dick made his bear slither in his head with want.

Shoving those feelings as deep as he could, he took off at a full run and burst into his animal the second he was past the first tree. He hadn't even had a chance to remove his pants. They were now flittering to the ground in denim confetti.

A glance back at the house and his bear made a strange purring sound. Piper was standing on the porch, her arms crossed over her chest, her lips parted, her eyes wide as she watched him. His bear wanted to turn back around and run to her, comfort her, touch her. The human side of him wanted so much more.

So, he ran. He pushed forward and ran deeper into the woods until he was confident Piper could no longer see him, but he could still see her house, still smell her, even past that ungodly chemical scent.

It was a fight the entire time he was away from Piper. Both sides of him wanted to run back to her, but Luke's rational side won. He was there to keep her safe, and he couldn't do that if he was lost in her eyes, her lips, her fucking body.

Chapter Five

Piper couldn't move. She literally couldn't will her feet to leave the spot on her porch. She could no longer see Luke, but she still couldn't move. She'd never seen anyone like him before.

He was big, she knew that from the night he'd pulled Barrett away from her and stood over like a shield. But this? What she'd just seen?

Piper wanted him to hang out with her for a while. She wanted to show her gratitude for everything he and his friends were doing and going to do for her. She wanted to make him dinner or something. Anything.

But Luke seemed to...shut down. She didn't know how else to explain it. When he'd complimented her house, she'd felt this little flutter in her stomach and couldn't help the smile that stretched across her face. He mirrored that smile and, for a brief second, looked so charming and kind of sweet.

And just as quickly as that smile appeared, it disappeared. Was he mad about their kiss? He'd been the one to kiss her. She simply hadn't bothered to stop it. Which she should have. It had just felt too damn good.

But now, her body was warmed all over again. Even more so than when she'd felt his rough kiss.

Luke was covered in tattoos. They ran across his back and chest, across his shoulders, down his arms, and onto his hands. She hadn't gotten a glimpse of his lower half. He'd still been wearing his pants when his bear had exploded from him. She'd never seen someone Shift so quickly. Had it hurt as badly as her Shifts did? Probably not. Not with as quick as it had happened for him. Hers seemed to take forever each time she let her cougar have her body.

It was more than just the tattoos, though. He was ripped. As in, there were muscles she didn't even know existed bunching and rolling with each step as he ran for the woods. The man was unbridled power. No wonder Barrett had been nothing for him that night. No wonder he didn't appear nervous about more than one male cougar showing up on her property.

Once she could no longer hear or see Luke's bear, which was even more massive than she remembered, Piper backed up until she hit her door. The thought of turning and giving an animal that big and fierce her back scared her. That was stupid, though. Luke would never hurt her. And she knew his animal wouldn't either. Or she hoped. Because there was no way her cougar would be a match for that beast.

Reaching behind her, she pushed the door open and slipped inside, then closed and locked the main door the second the screen swung shut. Leaning her forehead forward, she pressed her palms against the door and took a few deep breaths. She hadn't been ready for the reaction her body had to the sight of a shirtless Luke.

She felt like she was going insane. She'd known since she was a teenager she didn't want a mate. She didn't want to be tethered to anyone. She didn't want to give her freedom up to another living soul.

But, something about Luke made her feel different. Not only was she attracted to him on a crazy level, but she was having all these thoughts, thoughts of Luke in her bed, his hands on her body, his presence in her life on a regular basis.

As much as she hated the thought of being tied to someone, would it really be that bad to be tied to Luke? He was so…different. And not just because of the tattoos. A lot of people had tattoos. But he felt different. To both sides of Piper. Even her cougar had come out of the corners of her mind and paid more attention to Luke. She slithered around and purred when Luke was around. Shoot. She did that when Piper merely thought about Luke.

"Ugh!" Piper groaned as she pushed away from the door.

She had to stop thinking about Luke in that way. Although, now that she'd seen more of him, that was going to be pretty freaking hard. So pretty. No. That wasn't the right word to describe a man like Luke.

Aaaand she was once again obsessing. Looking around the room, she looked for something to clean or organize or anything to keep her hands and mind busy. But she'd cleaned the whole house while waiting for Luke to get there. And now he was there. And her house was clean. And he'd only seen the living room before rushing back outside.

Her mind decided that was the perfect time to replay their kiss. Kis*es*. Multiple. Two of them. Why not let her mind wander? How much could it hurt to wonder how it would've felt if he'd deepened that kiss or slid his hands up her back? Or her front?

Piper looked down at herself. She didn't really have much to fondle, but at least her breasts were firm and perky. Her chest was small, like the rest of her. She was proportionate. That had been her argument anytime her mother would tell her she was too skinny or her breasts were too small or her behind was too flat.

And talking back usually earned her punishment. But she never stopped. Never caved in. Never let anyone make her feel as if she shouldn't have a voice.

And no matter how many times Barrett or Andrew or her parents or anyone else tried to force her into something she didn't want, she'd never back down. They'd have to kill her.

Piper shuddered at that thought. The last visit from Barrett had been bad. So bad. When she'd woken on the floor, she'd wondered for a brief second if she was dead. Everything had hurt.

And two days later, she'd scented Luke on her property. And it had been more than just him wandering around; his bear had actually peed in her yard. He'd marked her territory. Marked his territory.

"Oh no," she breathed out, straightening from where she'd knelt in her closet to move her shoes around.

He'd marked his territory. He'd left his scent there as a warning. And she had a sneaking suspicion it was more than Barrett he was trying to warn away. He was trying to scare away other males. Was he even aware of his actions? Of course, she knew he was aware he'd urinated there, but was he aware of exactly why he'd done it?

Piper's heart raced as she mulled over all the current information overloading her brain. That was too much like mate behavior. And as resistant as she'd been to being paired up, something about Luke appealed to her in a way no one and nothing ever had. And her cougar absolutely noticed the big male. Especially shirtless.

Her body was still warm from the sight of all that masculinity on display. Every time she blinked, she could see Luke running across her yard, could see the moment his bear burst from his skin and shook out his fur.

Luke was out there somewhere, prowling the woods, watching out for her. Watching over her. That sense of security came over her again. Even with him hidden in the dark trees, she felt as if there were this big force field around her house, blocking anyone who wanted to force their crap on her.

And he'd kissed her twice.

Once again, she was circling right back to that. It didn't matter how hard she tried, she couldn't forget the way his lips felt against hers, the warmth of his breath, the sound he'd made in his truck. It'd sounded desperate. Or pained. Was it pained? Why would it sound pained? And why were her thoughts a little on the shrill side inside her own head?

More importantly, why couldn't she stop her thoughts from going round and round? She wasn't some boy crazy Shifter. She didn't mind the occasional hookup, but only with men she didn't know and knew nothing about her. Anonymity was key. No connections, no bonds, no feelings.

Would it be possible to sate a need with Luke without feeling a single connection? Would he be open to something like that?

No and no.

With a heavy sigh, Piper plopped down on her couch and dropped her head against the cushion. Why did she have to be so different? It would've been so much easier if she'd been born to please like the females in her Pride. Or born male. Although, they were forced into breeding females, as well. But at least they had choices and a life of their own outside of their mate.

Piper eyed the coffee table. It had been cleaned since Barrett put his filthy feet on it. And the sight of his big, muddy feet on her pretty furniture irritated her. But…he'd looked comfortable.

Like the weirdo she was, Piper glanced around as if someone would be there to see her. And then she lifted her bare feet and propped them onto the white top. Okay. This was kind of comfortable. Not something she could see herself doing on a regular basis; relaxing was done in her bed at night when she devoured a book for hours on end. Or until she fell asleep and the book fell on her face.

Something rustled outside of her house and she jerked her feet off the table, dropped them to the ground, and straightened her spine.

Watching the door, she was both excited and nervous as to who was out there. What if Barrett had gotten past Luke and was seconds away from barging into her house? What if he'd hurt Luke?

The thought of Luke in the woods injured and alone had Piper on her feet and running to the door within a half second. She yanked the door open and searched the open space for the source of the noise.

Nothing. There was literally nothing outside of her house. Must've been a squirrel bouncing around.

But she'd run outside ready to defend Luke from an unknown assailant. What did that say about her? What did that say about her feelings for Luke?

Again...nothing. She wanted to protect him the way he'd protected her. Nothing more.

Liar.

Piper jerked at the sound in her head. Since when did her cougar talk back? Since when did she even talk? Purr? Sure. Growl? Yep. But talk?

Okay. She'd heard thoughts from her cougar before, but nothing like this. Nothing so freaking assertive and aggressive.

"I'm not lying," Piper whispered.

Liar.

Whatever. She wasn't going to stand out there and argue with herself. Or her animal. Or both.

Her brain was mush. It had been a little on the mushy side since that first night. And then it got mushier the first night she hung out with him, actually walked beside him through the grocery store. Now that she'd spent a few hours with him, it was officially oatmeal-on-a-cold-night.

It didn't make sense. It was too...chaotic. Her thoughts, her life, her emotions, too out of control.

And there was nothing to clean.

She needed to Shift. To run through the woods. And maybe then she'd just traipse through the house in her animal form and track dirt across the carpet. *Then* she'd have something to clean, dang it. Cleaning always calmed her. Cleaning made sense.

All the rest of this, these feelings and confusion were messy.

Mind made up, she checked again to make sure no one was around to witness her nudity, stripped her cleaning clothes off, and folded them nicely before piling them on the porch rail. She waited until she was a couple yards away from her porch before she dropped to her knees and called to her cougar, giving her permission to take over for a while. At least long enough to expel some of the nervous energy.

Piper took off in the opposite direction where she'd seen Luke disappear. She didn't really want to run into him, not in her animal form. She had no doubt Luke's bear would be all powerful and dominant while she was...well, not submissive, really. Rebellious? That was a pretty good word to describe both herself and her cat. Although, anyone who saw the way she color-coded and alphabetized everything would disagree.

But when it came to Shifter behavior, she was rebellious. She refused to behave the way she was supposed to or expected to. Just because she had an animal inside of her didn't mean she had to act like an animal, dang it! She never let her cougar hunt prey, didn't find it necessary to leave her scent anywhere the way Luke had. Had never found it important to find a mate or breed.

Until Luke.

She still didn't exactly find it important to have a mate nor did the thought of carrying a live creature in her belly sound appealing, but Luke made her wonder how life with a true mate could be, how it could feel to be in the arms of someone who cared about her.

Just because Luke kissed her didn't mean he cared about her any further than her safety. It just meant he was a warm-blooded male and she was an available female.

Her cougar's paws hit the ground with dull thuds as she pushed her animal as fast as she could go. She inhaled the scents of the forest, the damp and mildewing leaves dropped to the ground with the passing fall, the crisp night air tickling her nose.

And the pungent scent of another predator.

Shit. Luke must've been circling her property instead of staying across the field. He was close enough she could not only smell him now, but here his chuffing breaths and the heavy padding of his massive paws. He would be at least three times bigger than her in his bear's form.

Piper slid to a stop and swung her head around, trying to gauge which direction Luke was coming from and which direction she should run. He wouldn't hurt her, but she didn't want the chance of their animals bonding the way their human forms had. That would be her luck - a mark from his bear when she was still Shifted.

Before she had a chance to turn on her heel and bolt back to her house, Luke's enormous bear stalked out from behind thick brush. He halted, almost looked surprised by her presence, then lifted his snout into the air and sniffed. When he was content it was Piper and not a threat, he dropped his head, doing this nod thing, and made a chuffing sound.

Piper was frozen in place again, just like she'd been on her porch. Luke's bear was ambling toward her, his paws hitting the ground hard enough she could feel it from where she stood. Her cougar wanted to drop to her belly and submit to the massive beast, but Piper wouldn't allow that. She'd never submitted to a male before and she wouldn't start with Luke.

Forcing her cougar to stay on her feet, she lifted her head and waited as Luke came closer, his nostrils flaring as he sniffed over and over again, like he was memorizing her scent. His animal was impressive, so big and scruffy, his dark brown fur nearly blending in to the dark forest around him.

And his eyes…they were the same whiskey colored eyes she'd come close to getting lost in several times today.

Now that they were face to face like this, Piper wished she was still in her human form. There was little way to communicate in their animal forms. She just awkwardly stood there as Luke's bear rounded her, his nose close to her fur as he breathed her in. Then, after a few minutes, he nudged her shoulder with his snout. What? Did he want her to go away? Go back to the house? Was there danger nearby?

Those reruns of *Lassie* she'd watched as a kid came to mind: What is it boy? Did Timmy fall in the well?

She couldn't speak and neither could he.

Turning in the direction he'd nudged her, she took a tentative step, then looked at him over her shoulder. He was walking with her, passing her as she waited to see what he wanted. Jogging, she caught up to his long strides and walked beside him. Then jogged again as his steps grew quicker.

And then they were running, their heavy breaths the only sound deep in the woods as they let their animals be free, ran and played the way she hadn't done…well, ever.

After a few minutes, Luke's bear swiped out a paw and clipped one of her legs out from under her. She stumbled then righted herself and caught back up. Oh, his bear wanted to race, did he? And the jerk didn't plan on playing fair. Well, two could play at that game.

Faking another stumble, she slowed, faked a limp, and whined. Luke skid to a stop and turned to check on her. When he started to make his way back to her, Piper took off at a dead run, passing him and releasing a feline scream into the air, her own little victory cry.

Whether she'd really won or Luke caught on and had let her win, she didn't know. And didn't care. All she knew, was this was the most fun she'd had in a long stinking time.

****

Piper was a beautiful woman. No doubt in Luke's mind about that. But her animal was…fierce. And scarred. So fucking scarred. There were lines crisscrossing her hind end. Yet Piper didn't bother hiding from him as he circled her, surveying every inch of her cougar's body. Was Piper permanently scarred in her human form? Or was this damage done when she was Shifted?

He'd always carried his wounds from battles on his human flesh, so there was no reason she would be any different. A murderous rage built in his chest. Until he got a real good look at Piper. She kept raising her chin and her legs were trembling, as if she were fighting her animals' instinct to drop to her belly in submission. Piper the human refused to be a victim.

Strong woman. He liked that. A lot.

Luke needed her to be comfortable with him in this form just as much as his human form. So he did the only thing that came to mind – he challenged her to a race.

At first, when he nudged her to move, she watched him with curious eyes. Until he started moving in the direction he'd tried to urge her to run. She began to follow him, a couple of feet behind him. But when he started jogging, she caught up and ran right beside him, the sounds of her paws hitting the ground silent compared to his.

The second he broke into a run, she was right there, pushing those sinewy legs to keep up, to beat him at this race. If he was in his human form, a smile as wide as he'd ever had would've been plastered on his face. His bear released a chuffing sound so much like a laugh it shocked the shit out of Luke. Even his bear was having a good time.

Her cougar was passing him. And he'd never been one to waste an opportunity, so he swiped out a paw and caught her back foot. She stumbled and he had a second of regret. He didn't want her to get hurt.

She slowed and began to limp, a low keening echoing against the trees. Fuck!

Luke skid to a stop and turned to run back to her. And the cheater took the opportunity and zoomed past him, a roar filling the air. She was laughing at him. Or celebrating her ill won victory. Not that he'd complain; he'd tried to cheat first.

His brave, fierce cougar turned and released another of those sounds and almost looked like she was smiling.

His cougar? Not his. Never his.

Luke immediately took his skin back and straightened.

Piper's cougar tilted her head in confusion, then she Shifted back to her human form.

"What's wrong?" she asked, breathless and laughing. "You're not a sore loser, are you? 'Cause you totally cheated first."

Luke's breath caught in his lungs and his heart rate tripled. Piper clothed was something special, if not a little stuffy. Piper naked was…

"Fuck," he muttered, then glanced down at himself when he realized her eyes were slowly roaming his body. He cupped his junk in his hand and lifted his gaze back to her. "Did I hurt you?"

Her smile faltered then fell completely. "No. I was just trying to you fake you out since you were obviously trying to cheat," she said. Her smile came again then fell when he didn't smile back.

But he wanted to. He wanted to continue playing with her, racing her in the woods, even wrestle her cat in the leaves. Yet that all felt too intimate. Like something he'd do with someone he had feelings for, which he didn't.

His bear growled in his head and the sound poured from Luke's lips.

"I was just…" She cut off her words and finally realized she was naked. One arm covered her tits while the other crossed over her lower half. But all the rest of that creamy, soft looking flesh was still visible.

And then something hit him.

"Turn around," he growled out.

"What? No way. I only have so many hands to cover myself," Piper protested.

Normally, nudity was nothing to Shifters. It was just part of the process during a Shift. But something about seeing Piper naked made his body tighten in places he had no right to think about.

"I'm not trying to check out your ass," he half lied. Only half. Because if she'd turn around so he could see if those scars he'd seen in her fur were across her lower back, ass, and upper thighs, he'd probably take the opportunity to see how firm she was back there, too.

"Right. I'm standing here naked. Why else would you want me to do a turn for you?"

A muscle ticked in his jaw as he clenched his teeth. "Turn around," he said again.

"And again, no."

This woman had been through hell and back, yet she refused to let anyone break her, to boss her around, to dictate her life for her.

And because his mind wasn't fucked enough, he realized how much he wanted her because of that.

"Your cougar had scars," he said after a few seconds of them trying to stare each other down.

"Yeah?" she said, her shoulders shrugging slightly.

"What are they from?" he growled out. Couldn't stop growling. He was having a hell of a time pushing his bear all the way to the back of his mind.

"Do you really need me to say it?" she said, crossing her arms over her chest, then dropping one arm back to the apex of her thighs when she remembered they were standing in the middle of the woods naked as the day they were born.

Yes. No. He wanted to know the truth, but feared if she said the words, if she gave him details, he'd abandon his post and hunt down every single mother fucker who'd ever laid a finger on her. And that included her own fucking father.

Her mother he'd have to leave to someone like Peyton. Her bat shit crazy wolf would love to tear into someone who hurt Piper. Or any female for that matter.

Luke shoved one hand through his hair while keeping his hand over his dick. "You should get back to the house. It's getting late."

"It's already late," she said with another of those small shrugs.

Luke's eyes betrayed him and dropped to the place where her hands covered. He hadn't meant to check her out, but he had. And he'd liked what he'd seen. And couldn't stop wishing she'd move her arms so he could look again.

He was a prick. A pervert. A fucking hypocrite. He was there to protect her, yet he wanted to stare at her tits and anything else she was willing to show him. It was a distraction neither of them could afford. If he lost himself in Piper, in her beauty, in her body, it would be far too easy for her brother or another member of her fucked up Pride to creep onto her property. He didn't give two shits if something happened to him, but he'd never forgive himself if anything ever happened to her.

Mine.

Luke started hard at the sound of his bear's voice in his head.

No. Fuck no. Not happening.

"Go home," he said, gritting his teeth against urges he wasn't sure was his own or his bear's. Maybe both.

He wanted to touch her. He wanted to see if her skin was as soft as her lips. He wanted to feel her small tits in his hands. He wanted to run his tongue across every inch of her body. He wanted to bury his dick and his teeth in her.

He wanted to mark her for life.

Chapter Six

Luke was looking at her funny. Not *ha ha* funny, either. And he was being a little on the bossy side.

"Go home," he growled out. He kept snapping things at her, asking her to turn for him, asking her about her scars. And that growl, it was nonstop as it trickled from his mouth.

And then something changed.

He twitched, as if something scared him. His eyes went wide, his lips parted, and, although she was trying not to look, the tip of his man parts peeked out over the top of his hand. He was turned on.

Well. She was a woman standing naked right in front of him. Natural reaction. Right?

So then, why did his growling stop so suddenly? Why were his eyes glowing so brightly? And why was he taking slow steps in her direction?

His hands were no longer hiding himself from her eyes. She got a full shot of all of him, from the dark tattoos across his chest, shoulders, and arms, the way a few snaked over his hip, the scars shining silver in the moonlight, so similar to hers, all the way to the impressive and slightly intimidating package he was sporting.

Luke was everything. He was everything she'd never wanted and everything she had to have. It was like something deep inside of her clicked into place and she knew she had to have him. She had to have him now and she had to have him for good. She wanted him in her house, not just in her woods. She wanted him beside her in bed, his hands trailing a hot path down her body.

Piper wanted to feel all of him pressing down on her from above.

Purring crept up her throat and trickled from her parted lips. Apparently, her cougar was on board, as well.

Moving toward him, she met him halfway, dropping her arms to her sides so Luke could see her body, too. Although, she was nothing compared to him. What did he think of her now? His lower half seemed to like the sight of her, but what about Luke's rational side? She was nothing like the women he knew. She didn't have curves for days, or big boobs. Nope. She was queen of the itty bitty titty committee. Or so she'd been told since she'd started puberty.

His hand raised in a jerky motion, like he was fighting himself. Instead of immediately cupping her breasts or sliding his fingers through her folds, he cupped the side of her face and dipped his head down to hers. He had to bend almost in half to kiss her, so Piper raised onto her toes and threw her arms around his neck, tilting her head and pushing them further with a swipe of her tongue across the seam of his lips.

He made that same pained sound he'd made in the truck, but he opened for her, touching his tongue to hers, tasting her, teasing her. His one hand still cupping her face, the other went around to her back and pulled her closer to him until his hardness was trapped between them, pressing against her belly, begging to be touched.

Without giving it much thought, Piper smoothed her hand down his rock-hard chest and circled her fingers around his girth. Luke immediately broke the kiss with a hiss though his teeth and pulled away, dropping his hands from her, putting a good foot of space between them.

"What?" she breathed out.

She might not be all about the mating bond, but she'd never been one to deny herself the carnal pleasures that came from the opposite sex.

Luke's face was scrunched up and he was holding his head in his hands, shaking his head and saying, "No," over and over again.

"What's wrong?"

There couldn't be a threat. There was no way Luke would fall apart or even falter if he thought someone was there to hurt her. She'd seen the wild look in his eyes that night, even if his eyes had been all she could remember.

"I can't," he said, finally dropping his fists to his sides. He was grinding his teeth. A muscle ticked in his jaw. She'd seen him do that a couple of times today.

"Can't what?"

"This," he said, waving his hand between the two of them.

"Why not?" She hadn't really meant to blurt that out, but now, her body was primed and ready to go and she wasn't looking forward to the discomfort she'd have from missing out on a little relief.

His brows pinched together tightly and his eyes flashed brighter. And then he was lunging at her, his hands tangling in her hair, his lips crashing onto hers. She gasped at his sudden movement and he took the opportunity to dip his tongue into her mouth again. His kiss was deep and bruising and exactly what she needed.

But just as quickly as it happened, it ended. He pulled away and stalked off into the woods without saying another word and Piper was left standing there, her fingertips touching her swollen lips, even more confused than she'd ever been in her life.

Piper's bare feet were tender by the time she'd made it back to her house. Pinecones and twigs and God only knew what else had bit into their soles with every step. Next time, she'd ask Luke to run closer to her house so she wouldn't have so far to walk back.

If there was a next time.

She had no idea what had happened or what had caused the torn look on Luke's face. But she knew it had to do with her.

I can't. What couldn't he do? She could tell he was physically able to close the deal, so that wasn't it. So then…what?

It was her. It had to be. He didn't want to make love to her. Although, that wouldn't have been what they would've done. They would've…fucked. Even thinking that word in her own head made her cheeks flush with heat. But that was the only way to describe a quickie in the woods with a man she barely knew.

Yet…she did know him. Or at least she felt like she did. She felt like her heart knew him, had known him since that first night.

Her cougar sure liked him. She'd slithered and purred nonstop in her head from the second Luke had Shifted back to his human form. The purr had even broken through her lips and into the quiet night. That sound seemed to do something to Luke. Gooseflesh had broken out on his arms and chest.

But she was walking into her house alone and frustrated. And not in the physical sense, although that was there, too. No. She was rattled. Scared. And so stinking disappointed.

Piper's body was on fire. Her lips tingled from where Luke had been pressed against her and his scent enveloped her. He'd been into her, into their kiss. So why did he break away so abruptly?

I can't.

Those two words banged around inside her head as she dropped her folded clothes into the hamper and shuffled to her bathroom. She hated to wash his scent off, but she always showered at night. And in the morning before work.

Would it be so bad to break her little quirk for the night? Would it be so bad to be wrapped in Luke as she drifted off to sleep?

Turning on her heel, she headed back to her bed. It wouldn't kill her to skip her evening shower. She'd just scrub harder in the morning. For tonight, she wanted to pretend she was normal, that she came from a normal family and had met a male who interested her enough to contemplate bringing him back to her bed. She wanted to pretend she actually had a choice about her life and future.

Sleep came fast, but it was far from restful. She tossed and turned every time she woke up, her mind instantly going to Luke and whether he was near her house when her brain would make the trek from dreams to reality. Even when she slept, she dreamed of Luke, of his kiss, of that body.

And what a body.

Piper had never thought of herself as someone who'd be attracted to tattoos, to a bad boy. And maybe Luke wasn't technically a bad boy, but he sure as heck looked like one. She had this urge to run her finger along every inked line on his body and follow it with her tongue.

What was this feeling? She'd been attracted to men before but she'd never felt...possessed. That's how it felt, like she'd been possessed by someone else or like she was losing her mind. She had no doubt sex with Luke would be explosive, but she'd been with men who were good in bed, too. It didn't make sense why his rejection would hurt so bad. And it did.

Even when she woke the next morning, she couldn't help but dwell on every single second she'd spent with Luke last night from the race to the mini make out session.

To the moment he'd shut down and looked terrified. No. That wasn't the right word. Definitely scared, but he'd looked more confused than anything. Pretty much how she felt for the last seven hours.

Was he still out there? Or had he gone home when the sun rose? He had to have slept at some point. Although, being Sunday, he was off and could sleep during the day. But that wasn't exactly a healthy life.

He'd been hanging out on her property for weeks before she'd confronted him. And then he'd come back and urinated in her yard. He could pretend he was being her bodyguard all he wanted, but she wasn't the only female dealing with an overbearing family. There were plenty of women out there who needed help. So… why her?

Piper didn't want a mate. Really, she never had. She wasn't opposed to entertaining the idea if she ever found her true mate and fell in love, but now, she couldn't picture her life without Luke in it. Maybe she could convince him to stay friends when all was said and done, when her family was finally out of the picture.

Although, being as this kind of stuff had been going on since she was young, she couldn't picture them stopping simply because of Luke's presence. They might step back for a while and wait it out, but they'd never go away. She'd always have to watch over her shoulder.

Or she could move, pack up and pick another state to land. No. She couldn't do that. Not only was that way too far outside of her comfort zone but there were risks in other states, males like her brothers who would try to force her into a life she didn't want. And then there were the traffickers, the low life jerks who stole women from their homes, from the street, wherever they could find them and sell them to the highest bidder. She refused to be a slave to anyone. *Especially* a stranger.

Luke wasn't a stranger. And her heart beat an unfamiliar cadence when she thought about him, and it was more than simply how he looked under his clothes. It was something about his energy, his strength, his loyalty to his people and to her. He was willing to put himself at risk and even call in his Clan and the wolf Pack to keep her safe. He was selfless. And, even if it had been fleeting, he'd been playful.

She wanted to see that side of him more. She wanted to see him smile, laugh, joke, and play. She wanted to Shift with him again and run through the woods, just the two of them and nature. It had felt so…perfect. The whole thing had been perfect.

And then it wasn't.

Throwing the blanket off, she stomped to the bathroom to shower and dress. She'd hunt him down today and find out what happened. If it was the kiss, she'd make sure it didn't happen again. She didn't want him to freak out every time they were around each other. She didn't want him to feel pressured into anything. She knew that feeling all too well.

After her long, hot as Hades shower, she dried her hair, smoothed it, applied her makeup, then headed into her closet to dress. She stopped just inside the door and took a step back, her eyes widening when she looked at her bed. It was unmade. For the first time in she didn't know how long, she'd actually left her room with her bed disheveled.

Her first instinct was to run over and straighten the whole thing out, smooth the bedspread and arrange the throw pillows in a perfect line. But why? Why did she have to?

"No. I'm in charge of my life," she said to her closet as she stepped back in and dropped the towel to the floor. Okay. That was too much. Piper scooped the towel from the floor, folded it, and laid it in the hamper on top of last night's clothes.

"Didn't say anyone else was," Luke's voice said from her bedroom doorway.

Piper screamed, whirled around to find Luke watching her, then slammed her closet door shut and locked it.

"What are you doing in here?" she called through the door.

"You left your front door unlocked last night," he said, his voice slightly muffled through the wooden door. "Don't do that again."

Piper grabbed the robe from the back of the closet door, slipped it on, then tied the tie around her waist, double knotting it to ensure it wouldn't slide open. She slid the lock out of place and peeked through the open door.

"What are you doing here? I thought you'd gone home."

He was leaning against the doorframe inside of her bedroom, his thick arms crossed over his barrel chest. He was dressed but barefoot. Had he taken his shoes off before coming into her house? Her eyes swept over her messy bed and she bit back a groan. Had she thought Luke or anyone else would've come into the house she would've made it the second she realized she'd flaked. Now, Luke was seeing her bedroom as a total mess.

"I'm heading home now. Emory and Eli are coming to hang out for a while. Then Micah and Callie. I'll be back tonight."

He turned to follow her line of sight and a crease formed between his brows. "What?" he asked.

Stepping all the way out of her closet, she hurried to the bed and started pulling it into place. Luke was there suddenly, fixing the other side. They didn't speak as they made her bed, but she'd caught him watching her, staring at her several times in the few minutes it took to make things right again.

"I, uh...I forgot to..." She waved her hand at the bed.

"I get it," he said, holding his hand up to stop her explanation. "It's a control thing."

It was her turn to frown at him. How had he known that? Did he have his own quirks she hadn't seen yet? She had a hard time picturing his big work boots lined up by color or style or his cereal lined up alphabetically, but maybe he had his own issues. That thought was mildly comforting.

Piper pulled her robe tighter at the collar, even though Luke had seen almost every inch of her body last night. Except her backside. Where the scars were. He might have seen them on her cougar, but she wasn't ready for him to see them in her human form.

Luke slowly moved toward the bedroom door, reaching his arms up and resting them on the frame. The motion brought the back of his shirt up enough for Piper to see a slice of his flesh. Tattooed. All of him was covered in art.

"About last night," he said with his back to her.

"Yeah. That," she said, eying her dresser that sat beside where he stood. She wanted to be clothed for this conversation. "Um…could you give me a second?"

He looked at her over his shoulder and nodded. "I'll be outside."

"You can wait in the living room," she said, forcing a smile on her lips. It was closed-lipped and tight, but it was the best she could do at the moment.

She had a feeling she knew how this conversation was going to go and couldn't muster up a real smile. Rejection and regret sucked. There were no ands, ifs, or buts about it. She'd rather be dressed when he looked her in the eye and told her what happened last night shouldn't have happened.

The second her door was closed, Piper hurried and pulled on a pair of panties, a bra, a pair of jeans – which she would normally only wear while cleaning – and a pink, cowl necked sweater. She was tempted to slide her feet into a pair of flats, but that would mean wearing her shoes in the house. Just because she'd gone a whole hour without making her bed didn't mean she was comfortable with tracking dirt across her pretty carpet.

Luke wasn't sitting on the couch or at the table when she stepped into the living room. He was leaned against the front door, his arms crossed over his chest again, his boots sitting on the tiled foyer floor beside his feet. She'd been right; he'd removed his shoes before coming into her house out of respect.

"Are you hungry? Can I get you some coffee?" she asked as she hurried across the living room and into the kitchen. She needed to keep her hands busy for this conversation. That would help keep her emotions in check and keep her from blurting out things she had no business saying.

"I'm good," he said. She looked back to see him watching her, only his eyes moving to track her movements.

"So…" Well, darn. She had no idea what to say now. She knew he wanted to talk to her about their impulsive behavior, but she wanted to at least attempt to stall as long as possible.

"I shouldn't have kissed you," he said when she was facing the coffee maker, her back to him.

She instinctively tensed. Yep. He was there to tell her she was all wrong for him, he didn't want a mate, didn't want to risk their forced friendship by throwing sex into the mix.

"It wasn't fair to you."

Okay. Maybe she'd been wrong about his exact motives, but it was still a rejection.

"I'm not...I can't have a mate. It wouldn't be right to do that to you."

Piper turned and frowned at him. When he continued to watch her silently, she leaned her back against the counter and rested her hands on the top. "Do what to me?"

Luke finally pushed from the door and moved slowly across the room, one jerky step after another, as if he was once again fighting his own body. Pushing his hand through his hair, he shook his head the same time his eyes dropped to her lips.

"I'm not mate material, Piper. I just want to keep you safe. I can't hurt you."

Piper's frown deepened. "How would kissing me hurt me, Luke?"

Of course, they'd been on a fast path to a whole lot more than kissing, but she left that part unsaid. It didn't need to be verbalized. He'd been there last night; he knew exactly what would've happened if he hadn't stopped them.

He stopped about five feet from Piper and crossed his arms again. It was a defensive position, like he was closing her out. Maybe he was trying to close the whole world out.

"My bear..." He dropped his head and stared at his feet as his toes curled into the carpet.

"I saw him," Piper said, her brows pulling together in confusion.

His lips quirked and he raised his head the tiniest and looked at her. "Your cougar is amazing."

"Thanks," she said, her lips pulling up in a genuine smile. "Your bear was pretty impressive, too."

He took another step toward her. "Last night, when we were racing..." Another step. "My bear..."

Finish the sentence, dang it. The suspense was killing her.

"Yeah?"

"He claimed you."

Piper's smile fell so fast she felt her ears move. That was not what she was expecting to hear him say. Those three words were literally the last thing she thought he'd say to her.

"What?" she breathed out. Her cougar had been pretty interested in Luke all along, but at no point had she thought those words in Piper's head.

Liar.

I am not. You've never said anything like that to me, Piper argued with her cougar internally. She might've purred and enjoyed the attention they were getting from Luke, but she'd never claimed the huge man or anything of the sort.

Luke's head was raised and tilted as he watched her internal struggle. His dark blonde brows were pulled together and his eyes were narrowed. He didn't look suspicious, rather understanding. Did he know she was fighting with her animal? Probably. He seemed to be struggling for dominance over his own animal, as well.

"Piper," he said, his voice so soft.

"Yeah?"

"What did she say?"

It was Piper's turn to narrow her eyes at Luke. She wasn't sure she wanted to divulge that information, not yet. She wasn't even sure she wanted to admit it to herself. Her cougar was trying to tell her Luke was hers. Her animal was trying to claim this male.

"Nothing. It's nothing," she lied, waving her hand through the air like she could wave the thought away. "If your animal claimed me…what does that mean for us?"

"It means I'll still be here at night, but I need to stay away from you."

He shoved his hands deep in his pockets and went back to studying the carpet.

He needed to stay away from her? Why? If his animal had claimed her and her animal claimed him, didn't that make them true mates? This wasn't something forced on either of them by some outside party. Although, it would've been nice to have the choice as to who she tied herself to.

But if the universe had to choose for her, she couldn't have asked for a better man than Luke.

"What's your last name?" she asked when she realized she knew so little about him.

"What?" he asked, jerking his head up and frowning at her.

"You know my last name is Donnell. What's your last name?"

His head tilted to the side. "Warner."

Luke Warner. Okay. At least she knew his last name. Not that it should matter, but since she knew their animals were trying to form a bond between them it was nice to know that much about him.

And now she didn't know what else to say. He'd pretty much told her whatever they might've begun to build was over. She'd said from the beginning she didn't want a mate. He'd said the same thing. Yet…the thought of Luke walking through her door and evicting himself from her life made her heart heavy.

She should say something. Tell him she'd had a change of heart. Tell him this wasn't something they were being forced into, that their animals had found their true mates for their human halves. Tell him that she'd work on her weird quirks and try to relax a little more. She should tell him she'd never been kissed the way he'd kissed her, that she'd never wanted anyone as badly as she'd wanted him from the first moment he'd stepped out of her woods and she'd gotten a good look into his whiskey colored eyes.

She did none of that. With a nod, she said, "Okay."

He nodded a few times, but he didn't back away from her, didn't turn and leave through her front door.

"It's safer for you," he said after a few awkward moments of silence.

"How? How would being mated to you be dangerous?"

The moment she'd said the word, her cougar stretched in her mind and purred so loud Piper almost couldn't hear her own thoughts.

Mine, her cat purred.

Too bad. He doesn't want us.

That didn't stop her animal, though. She kept watching Luke, waiting for him to come closer, waiting for him to do anything other than stare at Piper with sadness and longing and something else she couldn't decipher in those pretty eyes.

Luke shoved his hand through his hair again. It was a nervous habit, she realized. He did that when they talked about something he found uncomfortable.

"I just can't. I'm not...I can't be a mate, Piper. Especially not to you."

When she thought he'd leave, he crossed the space between them in three long strides, cupped her face in both hands, and pressed his lips to hers in a rough, bruising kiss. His breath was warm on her face. She balled her hands in his shirt, trying to force him to stay right there, but it didn't work.

Luke stepped away from her, letting his hands drop to his sides, then turned on his heel and left through her front door. Piper watched his back, watched as he closed the door with a glance back at her, so much pain in his eyes and in the lines of his face.

Her knees wobbled. She backed up until her legs hit a kitchen chair and dropped heavily onto it. Fingertips to her lips, she blinked back the tears that threatened to fall over her lashes.

Luke didn't think he could be her mate, but he refused to leave her unprotected. He was still sending his people to watch over her, still coming back tonight to keep her safe while she slept. Their animals were trying to bond, yet he was pushing her away.

But that kiss. It had held so many emotions, so much that it made her dizzy.

The rational side of Luke might not think he'd be good for her, but he didn't realize how much the soft click of her closing door had broken her heart. She was sure there'd never be another male she would connect to so deeply in such a short amount of time.

Bending at the waist, she wrapped her arms around her stomach and tried to will the pain of loss away. She didn't even want to clean. She wanted to curl into the fetal position on her floor and let the emotions sweep her under.

She knew without a single doubt in her twisted mind that she'd never feel for someone the way she felt for Luke.

And she'd already lost him before she ever had him.

Chapter Seven

Luke sat in his truck and waited until Emory and Eli pulled up Piper's driveway. He gave them a two-finger wave, then headed home. It didn't matter how hard he tried to pretend everything was normal, fine, like any other day.

His heart was sitting back there in that overly tidy, frilly house that smelled so much of Piper.

His heart had slammed in his chest when he'd spotted Piper's naked body in her closet, trying to find something to wear for the day. Since she hadn't heard him come in, he'd taken a moment to survey every inch of her body, counted every single one of those silver fucking scars across her lower back, her round ass cheeks, her thighs. Someone had whipped her. So many fucking times.

Murderous rage. That was what went through his veins as he realized how deep some of those scars had been.

And then she'd spoken.

When he answered her, she'd squealed and slammed the closet door shut, blocking his view of her body. She should've locked the door before bed, but if her thoughts had been as scattered as his after their almost fling, then he could understand her oversight of locking out the bad guys.

Or she slept secure in the knowledge Luke was just outside, ready to eliminate any threat. That gave him a boost of manly pride, but it still freaked him out to think of how easy it would be for anyone to get to her if he wasn't close enough.

He'd heard a soft click from the other side of the door; she had a lock on the inside. It was a safe place for her. She'd done that to give her some time if Barrett or some other fuck barreled into her house. Not that a simple lock and wooden door would stop a full-grown Shifter from breaking into her closet.

She'd finally emerged in a robe. Shame. He'd enjoyed ogling her, although he had no right. But he was a male with a healthy libido. Not that he'd done anything with it in years. More years than he'd liked to admit.

And now he had to tell her that he couldn't pursue whatever the fuck was going on between them. He'd come up with this great speech when he'd patrolled her property line, but now that he was standing so close with her scent wrapping itself around him and intoxicating him, the words stuck in his throat.

Piper eventually figured out the conversation wouldn't be a light and fun one and asked him to give her privacy to get dressed. He'd expected her to come out in another pair of slacks and one of those librarian cardigans she was so fond of. So when she came out in a pair of fitted jeans and a sweater, his mouth had gone dry.

Her hair and makeup were still done to perfection like every other time he'd seen her. Except last night. When she'd Shifted back to her human form his dick had gone instantly hard. She was breathless and chuckling, her cheeks had been flushed and her hair was tousled. Images of her with that tousled hair after a vigorous round of love making made him almost blow his load in his hand. Yeah. It had been that fucking long since the last time he'd been with a woman that he was ready to lose it over the beauty of his mate.

When he'd realized not only had his bear claimed the woman but he'd already begun to think of her as his, he'd freaked out. He'd seen the confusion and concern on her face when he'd told her to go home, but he couldn't risk being with any longer. If she'd stayed near, he would've laid her out on the forest floor and plunged deep into her warmth. That would just solidify the fucking bond he was trying to deny.

Telling her that he had to keep his distance from her had been one of the hardest fucking things he'd ever done. Because all he'd wanted to do was cross the space and kiss her until she was gasping for air then carry her into that girly bedroom and take her on her bed. He wanted to rumple the perfectly made bed and have her moaning his name.

He did allow himself one last kiss, though. He couldn't help it. He had to feel those soft lips once more before he went back to denying himself any form of connection to anyone other than his Clan.

"Fuck!" he bellowed in his quiet truck, hitting his wheel over and over until he feared he'd break the thing.

Even now, as he headed home to get some sleep before he headed back to Piper's, he had to fight his instinct to turn his truck around and run back to Piper. She'd felt it. She'd felt the connection. He'd watched as she twitched when, he assumed, her cougar had spoken in her head. Then watched the conflicting emotions cross her face as she argued with her animal. The joys of being a Shifter; it was like having multiple personalities at times.

Luke wanted Piper. He'd wanted her from the moment he'd seen her on that pavement, as fucked up as that sounded. He had no idea what the appeal had been at the time. She was terrified, her big doe eyes swollen and filled with tears. But there had been some mystical pull.

And now he knew.

The universe had chosen. His bear had chosen. His bear had recognized her, recognized her scent from the first second.

And he'd pushed her away. Like he'd continue to do. He couldn't mate her. He refused to be his father. Refused to put her and their future cubs through hell.

He knew because his father was a piece of shit didn't mean he had to follow the same path. But he'd rather be lonely and miserable the rest of his life than hurt someone he loved. He wouldn't risk it. Couldn't. Couldn't risk being an abusive piece of fucking shit.

The rest of his Clan, minus Hollyn and Noah, were home, their trucks parked outside their cabins. Carter and June sat on their porch.

"Any trouble?" Carter asked when Luke climbed out of his truck.

Luke shook his head, forced a smile for June, and headed inside. He was exhausted. His body, his mind, his heart, every hair on his body was dead tired. He needed a few hours of sleep before he headed back to Piper's at sunset. This time, though, he wouldn't announce his appearance. He'd relieve Micah and Callie, Shift, then head into the woods for the night. Problem with his nightly patrol, though, was the fact he had a manual labor job. He and his Clan owned a construction company. They were currently knee deep in building a ritzy new subdivision in Eureka. The income from that job alone would keep them comfortable through the slower winter months.

He'd be tired as fuck all day every day until he could ensure Piper's safety.

Luke stripped down to nothing and climbed under his blankets. It took him a few minutes to drift off, but mainly because he could hear Carter and June talking about him. They were worried. His entire Clan was. And he was sure the wolves had been talking, as well. They didn't need to worry. Nothing had changed for him.

Liar.

"Fuck you," he said to his bear out loud.

So some shit had changed. But only in his head. Nothing outside would change. When all was said and done and Piper had moved on and someday found a dude who could give her the world, he'd be right back where he was, alone and fucked in the head.

Mine, his bear growled in his head at the thought of Piper with another man.

Luke wasn't overly thrilled about the thought, either, but he wouldn't put Piper through bull shit for his own selfish needs.

Eventually, sleep quieted his restless mind and gave him a few hours of peace. He couldn't even remember whether he'd dreamed when his eyes finally cracked open.

The sun was still up, so he hadn't slept too long. But with the year coming to an end and winter right around the corner, the days were growing shorter. He'd always preferred the summer, preferred the short, warm nights to the long, bitterly cold ones.

Luke showered and put on some clean clothes…and then he wasn't sure what to do with himself. If he went outside, he'd be met with a game of *Twenty Questions*. Especially if Shawnee was outside.

Speaking of the little redhead, Luke wondered if she'd finally told her mate they were expecting a bundle of joy.

How much longer did he have before he had to choose between guarding Piper and guarding Shawnee? He knew there were enough eyes to keep Shawnee safe, but she was his family. She was a part of the Clan now.

Piper's our family, his bear said, taking the opportunity to twist the knife in Luke's gut.

"Fuck," he muttered as he shoved his foot into his boot.

He had to get out of his house. He couldn't sit there and obsess over every moment they'd shared. Which, in reality, weren't a whole lot. But every one of them had been loaded with so much intensity and desire.

Luke had a choice to make: He either sat in his house and banged his head against the wall to knock any thoughts of marking Piper loose from his brain or he went outside and got banged upside the head with constant questions and possible accusations. Not that any of the accusations would be malicious; Shawnee would accuse him of denying her of another sister and himself of happiness.

Both were probably true, although the last thing on his list of bull shit to deal with was whether or not Shawnee got another in-law. She needed to focus on her own growing family and stop worrying about the rest of them.

The lesser of the two evils was facing his Clan. They knew what was going on with Luke now, why he'd been constantly disappearing. They'd all volunteered their time to keep her safe, although, other than Luke, they'd all go in pairs. He didn't like the thought of Colton taking Shawnee on guard duty. She really, really needed to tell her mate about her delicate condition. Then, Luke wouldn't have to be the bad guy and demand she stay home.

Peeking his head out his door, he sighed with relief when he spotted no one. In fact, his truck was the only one still parked on the gravel. They'd all left without saying a word to him. His relief turned into suspicion – where the hell did they all go? Together? While he was asleep…

"Oh, hell no," he muttered and jogged to his truck.

He slammed it into gear and was halfway down the long gravel driveway before he pulled his seatbelt into place.

Those bastards were headed to Piper's. At one fucking time. What the hell were they thinking? She might be a strong, independent woman, but she was still suffering the effects of abuse. A group of Shifters approaching her at once would be too much.

Luke pressed his foot hard against the gas pedal, constantly checking the area for the police. The last thing he needed was to get pulled over for reckless driving. That would cost him time and a headache he didn't need. His license was faked, like any other identifying papers a human might view.

And just like he'd feared, there were not only two trucks from his Clan, but a few familiar cars from the Big River Pack, as well. He didn't see anyone in the yard, so that meant all those assholes were piled into her little cottage type house.

"Mother fucker," he muttered under his breath as he pushed his door open.

He was going to kick someone's ass. Piper was probably cowering in a corner, watching the clock, waiting for everyone to finally leave.

Luke didn't wait for an invite, didn't knock on the door. He yanked the fucker open and stormed into the house.

And froze in the foyer.

Colton, Carter, Gray, and Micah were all working on locks on Piper's doors and windows. Shawnee, June, Nova, and Callie were all huddled around Piper's bedroom door, laughing, smiling. He even heard Piper's soft laugh come from somewhere further in her room. She wasn't cowering. She wasn't hiding. She sounded like she was having fun. *Sounded*. That was the key word. He'd know the second he saw her eyes if she was overwhelmed.

Pushing gently through the crowd, and forcing a tight-lipped smile at the women, he stopped when he found Piper laying clothes out on the bed. She was holding a sweater in her hands, holding it up like she was inspecting it. It wasn't like her normal cardigans. It was more casual and looked soft.

Piper turned and looked over her shoulder, looked back at the sweater, then did a double take. Her big, green eyes were wide, her lips in a comical O shape. "Hey," she breathed out, her smile hesitant. "I didn't expect you for a few more hours."

And now Luke was standing in the doorway like a moron. He didn't know what to say. He'd been prepared to rush in and save the day and Piper was enjoying her time with his friends.

"I, uh…" *Think Luke*. Fuck. "I thought they were bothering you."

"How did you even know we were here?" Nova asked, pushing Luke aside and moving further into the room. "And that color would be *hawt* on you, girl," she said to Piper.

"What's going on?" Luke asked, crossing his arms over his chest and leaning against the doorframe.

"You realize your big body is blocking those of us who don't have a height advantage," Shawnee said, shoving Luke to the side. Or at least she tried to. She barely nudged him. But he moved out of courtesy, anyway.

"Nova went shopping," Callie, Micah's mate and a member of Big River, said.

"She needed some new clothes," Nova said with a shrug.

"Her clothes were fine," Luke said and tried to ignore the rush of pink on Piper's cheeks. "Do you want them to leave?" he asked.

Piper's light brows pinched together. "No. Why would I?"

"Aren't they –" He turned and motioned to the women standing around him, but soft-spoken Callie spoke up and cut him off.

"I asked if she was okay with it before I called Shawnee," Callie said.

"Shawnee called me," June said.

"I got a text from Micah that your girl here needed new locks," Colton said.

"She's not my –"

"And after seeing her outfit at Moe's, I figured it was the perfect opportunity to go shopping," Nova said.

"You always find an opportunity to go shopping," Callie teased.

"I just wanted to hang out for a bit," June said with a shrug. "It's my day off. I wanted to get out of the house."

"It's fine, Luke," Piper said, setting the new sweater back on the bed. "Although, you really didn't have to get all this," she said to Nova. "I mean, thank you. I haven't gotten any new clothes in years. It feels like my first Christmas."

Everyone stopped moving, stopped talking, and turned to gape at Piper. Even Luke was staring at her as if she'd started speaking in tongues. He'd had a shitty childhood, but he'd had Christmas every year. His mom would sneak money after each grocery shopping trip and get him and his brothers something. It was usually something small, but it was still a gift.

Piper had never had that? She'd never opened a gift or experienced the holidays? He wasn't overly sentimental or into all the hoopla of the holiday season, but everyone deserved to experience it at least once.

As the women went back to discussing cow necks or cowl necks or whatever the hell they were talking about, Luke looked over his shoulder at the guys. They could give her a Christmas. They could keep her safe and still put up a damn tree complete with lights and ornaments. Why not?

Mate.

Luke stifled a growl and left the room and the women to their girl talk. Instead of dwelling on that single word from his bear, he focused on the locks the men were installing. He jumped in and helped secure her house even further. They'd all be taking turns hanging around her, but this was one more layer of protection for the woman he couldn't deny he wanted more than anyone in his sad fucking life.

He couldn't do it. He couldn't risk it.

But what if...

What if he was able to be a good man? A good mate to Piper? What if he didn't turn out like his dad? He'd spent his entire life protecting women and those he cared about, so why would he suddenly turn into a woman beater? He hadn't spent much time around kids other than the cubs of Big River, but even then, it wasn't like he carried either of the little girls around or played with them. He had no idea how he'd be with children of his own. But he knew sure as fuck he'd take himself out before he ever hurt a kid.

"What about an alarm system? In case one of us is deeper in the woods?" Carter said, rubbing the back of his neck.

"Or we could all just stay closer," June, Carter's mate, offered from the doorway with a wink for her man.

They were all so mushy and lovey dovey all the time. It made him sick. Or it used to. Now, he found himself mildly jealous of what all his friends had. He wished he could be like them, wished he could find love so easily, wished he could trust himself enough to invite a woman into his heart and home.

****

Piper kept one eye on the clothes Nova had brought in several bags and one eye on her open bedroom door. The sight of Luke had surprised her, and honestly, unnerved her a tad. After their little…episode last night, she hadn't really expected to see him at all. She'd assumed he'd Shift the second he pulled in and stay in the woods. Not that she expected that. She would've given him the spare bed if he'd stayed in the house with her instead of running away at the first sign of intimacy.

She was a little salty today. More than a little. She was irritated, more at herself than Luke. What was she thinking throwing herself at him like that? He was trying to be kind and she pressured him into something he didn't want. Something she'd originally never wanted.

For some reason, though, she wanted him even more while her cougar had retreated into Piper's mind over the fact their mate – and she could be honest with herself that he was definitely her true mate – didn't want her back.

What did that say about her that his rejection made her want him more?

That didn't sound right, even in her own head. It wasn't the rejection; it was the sadness. He wanted her. She could tell he wanted her, but there was something holding him back. He'd looked so sad when he'd walked away from her. He'd looked so torn, as if it physically hurt him to walk away from her, to deny himself happiness.

But really. Could she make him happy? Even now, with all these people showing her kindness and bringing her gifts, she was already thinking about how much cleaning she'd have when they all left. She'd have to organize all her new clothes, find a place in her closet, make sure they were organized by color and style.

How could that kind of craziness make anyone happy? It would just make them…well, crazy.

Luke's voice rumbled from the other room and she shook her head at the sigh she released.

"Uh oh," someone said from behind her.

Piper turned to find all four women smiling at her.

"What?" she asked with a confused frown.

"We heard that," Nova said.

"Heard what?"

Nova clasped her hands in front of her, batted her lashes, and sighed dramatically. "That," she said as she dropped her hands back to her sides.

"What? I was just breathing."

They all looked at each other, stepped further into the room, then closed her bedroom door.

"Spill," June said.

"There's nothing to spill," Piper said, folding one of her new sweaters and setting it on the stack she'd already folded.

"Bull," Shawnee said. "He's been disappearing for weeks. And then we find out about you. There's definitely something to spill."

"I didn't even know he was out there at first," she lied. She'd known. She merely had no desire to tell these women she barely knew that she'd liked him out there, liked the thought of the big bear guarding her while she slept.

"Okay. This is getting kind of hot," Nova said, crossing the room and sitting on the end of Piper's bed.

Piper's anxiety spiked at the sight of her pretty comforter rumpling and creasing beneath Nova but she kept her mouth shut. She could nonchalantly fix it as they were leaving the bedroom.

"You think everything's hot," Callie teased Nova. When she caught Piper's confused look, her smile widened. "Nova writes sex books."

"Seriously?" Piper whisper screamed, her hand going to her chest as her brows shot up her forehead.

"I do not. I write romance books. That just happen to have some sex in them."

"A lot of sex," June interjected.

"And women eat them up. Hence the reason I'm able to afford my new bestie some new duds."

"Bestie?" Piper asked. Her face grew hot. She hadn't meant to sound so excited at the thought of a new best friend. Or any friend for that matter.

In a matter of days, she'd gained a slew of new friends who were now crowded in her house, bringing her gifts, securing her home, and putting her mind at ease about her future.

Or at least until they got bored with babysitting her and went back to their own lives. She'd deal with that bridge when she crossed it.

Hopefully, she'd win them over and they'd at least want to stay in contact with her. Honestly, her life was lonely. She'd been on her own against her Pride for so long, no one to talk to, no one to confide in. Not even a dang goldfish to keep her company.

Until Luke had come along.

Mate. The sound her cougar made around that word was sad and pitiful. And Piper knew the feeling. As each minute passed with Luke in her space, she wanted to stomp out there and demand he acknowledge what was happening between the two of them.

"All I know is I haven't seen Luke so talkative in…well, ever. Nova? You've known him the longest," Shawnee said, turning to the woman looking around Piper's room.

"Luke? He's never been much of a talker," Nova said. "He got worse after that deal with Emory, though."

"What deal?" Piper asked then wondered if she wanted to know the answer.

Piper had met Emory. She was one of the women who was supposed to accompany her mate over when Luke was at home. She wasn't sure she wanted to know if Luke had had an affair with her then have to look her in the face and pretend everything was fine. Because that would so not be fine. Already, she could feel green fog slither through her belly at the thought of Luke touching or kissing another woman the way he had Piper last night.

"You've met Emory, right?" Nova asked.

"Yeah. At Moe's. She's supposed to be over later." Would she still come over, though, if Luke was already there? And did he plan on staying or coming back later?

"Well, when she first mated with Eli, he was the Alpha of a Pride. A piece of crap Pride, too," Nova explained. "The people there were…reluctant to have Eli leading them. Not all of them were bad, I guess. But there were enough to cause problems. Well, one of the assholes there turned out to be from the Pride where Emory was sold to and –"

"She was sold?" Piper asked. Her parents had been trying to force her into pairing since she'd been old enough to get knocked up, but at least she hadn't been sold off like a damn cow.

"Yep. The guy she was supposed to mate with was an asshole. She eventually kicked his butt and ran away and ended up with Gray and the guys at Big River Pack."

"I thought she was a wolf," Piper said, lowering to sit beside Nova.

"She is. But her parents wanted her in a powerful Pride in hopes of increasing their army or something stupid like that. Anyway, a guy from her former Pride ended up being in Tammen. He wanted her to come back to the original Pride and thought she should be carrying a lion cub, not a bear cub. He tried to—" Nova cut herself off and shook her head. "He ended up slapping her around and was caught before he could rape her. But Luke was on guard duty that day. The bears and wolves were taking turns hanging out with her when she was home and Eli was at work. Luke blames himself to this day for what happened to her. Over a year later."

"Wow," Piper breathed out. The other women were a mixture of sad and angry. She had to assume they weren't angry at Luke. That wasn't his fault. "Is that why he said he can't be a mate?" she asked, narrowing her eyes and brows as she looked from woman to woman.

They looked to each other as confused as Piper felt. "I didn't know he said that," Shawnee said.

"Oh. Oh please don't tell him I told you that. He'll never trust me again."

"Girl. Calm down. No one's going to say jack. Are we girls?" Nova said.

They'd been whispering the whole conversation and the guys were still out in her living room hammering and running drills. Hopefully, they hadn't heard any of that conversation. She didn't want Luke to feel like she was betraying his confidence, not after everything he'd done for her.

"Just pretend I never said anything," Piper said, looking at the closed door as if she could see through it.

The women all promised to stay quiet. And eventually, they all left. All but Luke.

"I thought your other friends were coming over today," Piper said, sitting, then standing, then sitting again. She wasn't sure what to do with herself now that she and Luke were alone in her house.

Last time they were alone, she'd offered her body and heart up on a platter and Luke had turned up his nose. Well. Not really. He'd taken a sample *then* rejected her.

Shoot. What if it really was Piper he didn't want? What if it had nothing to do with him not wanting a mate and he just didn't want *her* as a mate?

"Are you hungry?"

"Why are you always trying to feed me?" he asked and his lips quirked up a little. Just a little, but it was there. He was teasing. Or amused by her need to feed him.

"Well, for one, you're always running around for hours. I assume you're not hunting and eating wild animals. If your metabolism is anything like mine, you've got to be starving after a while. And two, you've been nice to me. I want to be nice to you."

His face softened. And that hint of a glow was back in his eyes.

"I was abused," he blurted out.

Piper's breath caught in her lungs.

She didn't know what to say so she sat there quietly and let him speak. He continued to stand with his legs shoulder width apart and his arms crossed over his chest. Defensive position.

"My dad. He abused me and my brother and my mom. His dad was the same way. I guess his was the same, too. I come from a line of woman and child beaters."

Piper's mouth opened but nothing came out. She still couldn't think of a single thing to say. She wanted to offer him comfort but didn't know what he needed. She could tell in the short time she'd known him he wasn't the kind of guy who'd want or accept pity, so she tried to keep that out of her eyes.

The anger she felt at someone hurting him…she let that show and was sure her eyes were a bright mossy green as he spoke.

"I can't be like them. I can't hurt you."

"Oh." *I can't.* He thought he couldn't mate someone because he'd end up hurting them. He thought he'd end up hurting Piper if they mated. "Luke—"

"But I want to. I mean, I don't want to hurt you. I want…I stopped us last night because I knew what would happen if we let it go any further. I've never wanted anyone as badly as I want you. I haven't been able to stop thinking about you since that night in the parking lot. You've become like a ghost I can't shake."

Piper's heart raced at a painful rhythm and her blood was hot in her veins. Every muscle in her body burned to lunge to her feet and throw herself into Luke's arms. She wanted to feel him against her body, but more, she wanted to hold him, to console him, to assure him he could never be like his dad.

Luke's head dropped and he shuffled his bare feet on her carpet. "That's why I said I can't. It's not that I don't want to." His head raised enough for Piper to see his eyes. "I really want to. I just can't risk it, Piper. I'd rather die alone and miserable without you than risk ever laying a finger on you."

She couldn't take anymore. She couldn't sit there and let him beat himself up over something he hadn't done, would never do, and for things that were out of his control. She had a feeling some of his inner angst was over the fact he wasn't able to protect his mother when he was a child. But that was the thing, he was just a child. There would've been no way a cub could've stood up to a full-grown bear Shifter and not end up with a slew of scars. Or dead.

Piper was halfway to Luke when she froze and her eyes dropped to his covered torso. She'd seen scars lining his body. He even had one on his face. Were those from his childhood? Or from battles with other Clans, other Packs and Prides through the years?

She opened her mouth to ask then clacked it shut. Now wasn't the time. Already, she could smell fur, she could feel his turmoil from where she stood. His pain and anger rolled from him in waves as he watched her advance slowly.

When she was within touching distance, she raised her hand. And then couldn't think of anything to say to erase what was eating him up from the inside. She couldn't erase his memories, couldn't rewrite his past.

All she could do was be there for him now and help him to see the person she saw when she looked into his beautiful eyes.

"I like your friends," she said when she had no other words. He grunted in response. "Why did you think all of them would freak me out?"

He shrugged his shoulders up and leaned into her touch when she cupped his jaw.

"There are a lot of them. And you've been through hell."

"They've never hurt me, though."

"You seemed nervous around the guys at Moe's." He finally dropped his arms to his sides. One hand moved forward as if he wanted to touch her, but fell back and away from her.

"I was. But you were there. And you wouldn't keep anyone in your life who would hurt me. Or anyone else. I knew they had to be good people."

"Why?"

It was her turn to shrug. "Because you're a good man, Luke. Only a good man would sit outside my house night after night, even before you knew me, just to keep me safe. You were putting yourself in danger's way doing it. And I know you have to be tired. Yet, you kept showing up. To keep me safe." Piper took a step closer. "You're not your father, Luke. You could never be like him. What he did? What his father did? That makes them monsters, not you. It's not hereditary like your animal. They had ugly inside of them, something they couldn't control that made them lash out at the people they were supposed to protect. I see you, Luke. You don't have ugly inside of you. You have warmth and light and so much love to give. Don't die alone and miserable because of your father's sins."

Luke's arms snaked around her and pulled her to his chest so fast Piper gasped in surprise. And then those warm, soft, strong lips were on hers again. This time, she wasn't going to let him push her away.

Chapter Eight

Piper's lips parted on a small gasp. Luke took advantage and swiped his tongue inside, reveling in the satiny softness of her mouth, of her taste, of the helpless little moans she kept making as she threw her arms around his neck and pushed herself closer to him. It was like she was trying to climb his body and, fuck, he wanted her legs wrapped around his waist.

As gently as he could, he ran his hands down her sides, cupped her small, firm ass, and urged her thighs up and apart. He didn't have to urge much. The little librarian instantly wrapped her legs around him the second he lifted her from the ground.

Her fingers were tight in his hair, the tugs causing just enough pain to be pleasurable while still keeping him grounded. He wanted her. Fuck, he wanted her so bad he was shaking.

As Luke carried Piper to the couch and sat with her straddling him, her core settled directly over his rock solid dick. He wasn't sure he'd ever been so fucking hard in his life. He was achy with the need to slam balls deep into her. But he wouldn't. Would never. Not with Piper. She deserved gentle and sweet.

Two words that could never describe him.

Then, there was the other issue. It had been years since he'd been with a woman. He knew it was like riding a bike, or something instinctual, but for his first time with Piper, he wanted everything to be absolutely perfect.

Nerves caused things to happen to his body that was not supposed to happen. Not now. Not when he had a beautiful woman straddling him and rocking her hips against him.

And unfortunately, she'd noticed.

Piper pulled back and looked down between them then up to his face. Something passed through her eyes: embarrassment. Or maybe doubt? He wasn't sure.

"What's wrong?" she asked, stilling her hips from their tempting dance.

No way could he voice his thoughts. His fears. He just dropped his eyes and shook his head.

"Oh," she said, the sound so soft and heartbreaking. She began to climb off his lap; Luke grabbed her by her hips to keep her right where she was.

"Where you going?"

"You...I get it. It's okay. I know I'm not..." She shrugged. "Beautiful. Like your friends."

His hands gripped her hips harder and his shaft bounced right back to life. Pushing his hips upward, he smirked. "Does that feel like I'm not into you?"

Her eyes rolled back in her head for a brief second before she opened them and looked into Luke's face.

"Then what's wrong?" She pulled her bottom lip between her teeth and chewed it and Luke's attention was drawn straight to her mouth.

Shit. She needed his honesty. No matter how humiliating it was. No matter how hard it was for him to admit to her, to the woman his bear was clawing at his brain to mark.

"I just..." Why couldn't he form the words? If they were going to truly explore this thing building between them, he needed to be upfront with her. Help her to understand what was standing between them and total bliss.

"What, Luke?" she whispered, her soft, slender hand cupping his jaw the way it had earlier.

He loved her touch. Loved the gentleness of her hand. Loved her.

Realization hit him so hard he was dizzy. He'd been fighting the mate bond so hard he hadn't even realized his bear wasn't the only one claiming her; his heart was hers. Where she should've been weak and broken, the abuse she'd suffered had made her stronger. She was how he should've turned out. She was everything he wanted to be.

She was everything.

"I haven't had sex in six years. And it was only once," he admitted before he lost the nerve.

Her brows flew high up her forehead, her eyes went wide, and her mouth made this little O.

"So you're kind of a virgin," she said rather than asked. Her brows lowered and a sexy smile pulled her lips up. "I'll be your first."

"You'll be the only one who matters," he said, keeping his voice soft to avoid breaking the magic of the moment.

Her smile widened and her eyes softened. She leaned forward and brushed a kiss to his lips, a soft caress full of so much, of so many emotions.

When Piper pulled away, he swore he could feel his soul stretching, reaching for her, trying to bring her close again.

"We can go slow. We don't have to do anything tonight," she said, cupping his face in both hands now.

Wasn't that what he was supposed to say to her? Wasn't he the one who supposed to comfort her?

He'd spent so much time over the last few weeks seeing her as this weak, fragile woman, he hadn't bothered to realize all that shit her family had put her through had turned her into a warrior. Where she should've recoiled at another man's touch, she'd learned to appreciate those who were kind to her. She should've been afraid of Luke, of his male friends, but she trusted him, therefore, trusted his friends.

All the bullshit her Pride had put her through had made her one strong fucking woman. She hadn't let the scars on her backside define her, hadn't let herself be known as nothing but a survivor of abuse. She'd taken the licks and grown. She'd used each hit, slap, punch, everything they inflicted upon her and used it as fuel to build her life.

"Your clothes," he said, narrowing his eyes.

"What about them?" She pulled away a little and frowned.

"I want them off," he said and let the wry smile stretch across his face.

Piper's frown faded and a sexy, soft smile fell into its place. Still cupping his face, she pressed her lips to his again. This time, it wasn't chaste or sweet. It was firm and hungry. Her tongue tentatively touched the seam of his lips and he opened up and invited her in. The kiss quickly turned desperate and needy. Her hands left his face and ran down the sides of his neck, to his chest, his abs, then back up, leaving his muscles tensing under her touch.

When Piper pulled away, she was panting. "You're trembling," she whispered, her eyes bouncing between his.

"I'm nervous," he admitted. "I don't want to disappoint you."

"You couldn't." She pressed another kiss to his lips, then another.

And then, she took control of the situation. Instead of forcing him to jump into something he hadn't done since he was a teenager, she took the reins and let him off the hook. If she was in control, he couldn't technically disappoint her.

Unless he blew his load too early. Which, if the tightness already present in his balls was any indicator, was a distinct possibility.

Piper's hands ran down his chest again, hooked the hem of his shirt, then pushed it up, her hands warm and soft on his body. He leaned forward and lifted his arms so she could pull it over his head. She folded it, then set it on the couch beside them.

Luke frowned at his folded shirt. Was she going to fold each piece of clothing as they took them off? Was this part of that control thing of hers where everything had to be situated in a certain way?

So be it.

Grabbing the bottom hem of her shirt, he pulled it over her head, revealing small perky tits covered in a thin, cotton bra. He folded it the best he could and set it on top of his.

She watched his actions with her lip between her teeth.

"What?" Had he not folded it nicely enough.

"You don't have to do that. Only one of us needs to be crazy," she said. And then her smile was back. "I know I'm a little odd. But it makes me feel better when things are clean and organized." She shrugged up her slender shoulders.

"You don't have to explain anything to me," Luke said, splaying his hands along her back and pulling her close again.

And just like that, the magic was back. She kissed him into a stupor until he was gasping for air and rocking his hips up against her. She was rolling her hips to the same rhythm he was pumping against her.

He remembered this kind of stuff. He'd done plenty of dry humping as a teenager when he'd had his first girlfriend and they sneaked off to make out. She'd been his first and only. And the reason he'd stayed celibate for so fucking long.

Even the sounds of memories clanging around inside of his head didn't tamper his desire for Piper. In fact, she was pushing those memories away, drowning those sounds out, making him forget all the reasons he hadn't wanted to sleep with anyone or have a mate.

Piper pulled Luke's hands from her back and lifted them to her tits, holding them there for a second before leaning forward to take his lips again.

Heaven. He was in heaven. There was no other way to describe it. No. She didn't have big tits like his Clan brothers' mates, but hers were perfect to him, fit perfectly in the palms of his hands. And he had a feeling they'd fit perfectly in his mouth.

He had to know. He had to know how she tasted.

Luke struggled with the clasp at her back, unable to release the fucking strap of fabric keeping him from what he wanted.

She pulled away with a soft giggle and clicked something on the front of her bra, then shoved it off her shoulders, revealing two soft mounds with dark pink nipples all pebbled and begging for his lips and tongue.

Who was he to deny her?

Leaning forward, he lapped at one nipple while fondling her other tit. Piper threw her head back with a moan and arched her back, giving him full access. He sucked her hard nipple between his lips, gave it the softest bite from his teeth. Her fingers tangled in his hair and held him there, held him to her chest.

Moving to the other side, he gave her other nipple equal attention, licking, sucking, nipping. His name, whisper soft, escaped Piper's lips like a prayer.

With shaky hands, Luke reached between them and undid her pants, slowly popping the button and pulling the zipper down. He wanted to give her plenty of time to stop him in case she changed her mind and decided they were moving too fast.

He'd stop if she wanted him to, but he was pretty sure he'd go blind from jacking off when he got home.

Rising onto her knees, Piper climbed off his lap long enough to push her jeans down her legs and kick them off. Just like her shirt, she folded them and set them on the shirts. And then she was standing before him naked, watching him, as if she were waiting for his reaction to seeing all of her.

Did she really think he wouldn't want her now? Even the faint scars on the sides of her hips were appealing, not because of how they'd gotten there, but because of how strong they'd made her, who they'd made her become.

Luke gasped softly when she dropped to her knees between his and went to work on his pants. He lifted his ass when she began to tug at the hips. And then they were both naked.

Grasping him in her hand, Piper dipped her head as if to take him into her mouth. Nope. Not happening. He didn't want his first time with her to be too short and there was a good fucking chance he'd blow in her mouth within seconds.

"I want nothing more than your mouth on my dick, but I don't think I have enough control. Not yet." He smiled self-deprecatingly. "It's been too long."

Her smile was wicked as she continued to lean forward and ran her tongue from the base of his cock to the tip. Luke gritted his teeth so hard he waited for a molar to crack. Hissing through his teeth, he stopped her when she leaned forward to do it again.

"Piper," he warned with a smile.

She straightened away from him but stayed on the ground. "Do you have protection?" she asked.

Protection? Oh. Shit. A condom. He actually did have a rubber. It'd been in his wallet forever. Did they have expiration dates?

"In my wallet. Back pocket."

She rifled through his pants, pulled out his wallet and handed it to him, finally climbing to her feet to climb back on his lap, throwing one leg over him.

Still shaking. He was still fucking shaking. His hands fumbled with the pockets of his wallet until he located the gold wrapper and pulled it out. Ripping it with his teeth, he lowered it to his shaft.

"Here. Let me," she said, a wicked smirk on her face as she slowly rolled the rubber down his length and then squeezed.

Luke's eyes rolled back in his head as he dropped his head against the cushion and let her truly and completely take control.

Piper lifted and positioned the head of his dick to her sex, then lowered slowly, one hand gripping him, the other on his chest to keep her balance.

When he was fully sheathed deep inside her warmth and he was clenching his teeth and breathing heavy to hold back the explosion, Piper halted her movements, cupped his face and kissed a path from his lips, down his jaw, to his throat, right over the spot where bears mark each other. Did she know that? Did she know how sensitive that spot was or how badly he wanted her to latch on as she rode him and mark him for life?

In a few weeks, this woman had burrowed into his life, his heart, his soul, and he wanted to make her his for good. But he had to be sure. He had to be sure he wouldn't hurt her when he was enraged. He had to be sure he could treat her like the queen she was.

Within a few seconds, Luke was able to open his eyes and relax his jaw. He cupped the back of Piper's head and began to roll his hips. Fuck. He'd never felt anything so good in his life. She was tight and wet and warm and he was right back to clenching his teeth.

"Relax," she breathed against his throat. "If you go early, we'll just do it again." She pulled back and grinned at him with a wink.

They could do it again. And again. Hell. They could have sex as much as they wanted.

No more holding back.

Gripping her hips, Luke pushed up into her and she arched her back. Her hips made circles as she rode him, drove him deeper inside, chased her own orgasm as she leaned forward so his pubic bone pushed against her clit.

He would go too early. He knew that. But when they were done, he had every intention of spreading her out before him and making love to her with his mouth until she was crying out his name.

Piper's back was arched, her hands on his knees, her head thrown back as she continued to rise and fall on Luke's dick. They needed to slow down. He would absolutely take care of her if he went early, but he wanted to savor this, enjoy it as long as possible. This was the first time he'd make love to the woman his heart called home.

And he sure as fuck wasn't going to take it for granted.

But for all his efforts, he already felt the first tingles as his balls tightened.

"Fuck. Piper. Slow down," he gritted out.

"I can't," she said with a moan. "I'm going to…" And then her lips parted and the sexiest sound he'd ever heard left her mouth.

That was it. That was the moment he lost himself in her. Lost control of his own body. Pulling her closer, wrapping his arms around her waist and burying his face between her tits, he barked out his release as she kept riding him, drawing out his orgasm until he thought he'd pass out.

Luke gasped in breath after breath, his face still pressed to her now damp skin. Her fingers began to thread through his hair, her nails scraping his scalp as her heart thundered against his ear. Her sex was pulsing around him, and astoundingly, getting him excited again. He was still hard inside of her, but now, a second round of need was building.

Would he ever tire of her? Would he ever have a day where he was too tired to make love to her? Hell no. Not a chance. He'd waited his whole life to find peace. He'd just never thought it would come in the form of a thin, brown haired librarian.

Piper was still panting. She didn't pull away from him or raise off his lap. Would she be up for round two so soon? And would his condom be any good for a second release? He was pretty sure he'd filled that thing past its capacity and doubted it could hold anymore.

"Hey, Piper?"

"Yeah," she said softly.

"Any chance you have any condoms?"

A soft giggle met his ears through her chest.

"I think I have a couple in the bedroom. Why—oh," she said when he pushed his hips up and his dick further into her. "Wow! Already?"

She pulled away and looked into his face with a smile. Her cheeks were flushed, her lips pink and kiss swollen. She was stunning like this, all wild and vulnerable. And all his.

Carefully, Luke scooted to the edge of the couch and stood, keeping himself buried inside Piper with her legs wrapped around his waist, and carried her down the hall to her girly bedroom.

Piper released a cute but frustrated groan when he pulled from her to remove the first condom.

"Don't worry. I have a few other things in mind."

He pulled her until her ass was at the end of the bed and put her feet on his shoulders. Maybe he was inexperienced, but he wanted to taste Piper, needed to taste all of her. As he swiped his tongue through her folds, she dropped back against the bed and breathed heavily, releasing soft moans, letting Luke know he was doing something right.

He had every intention of making love to her several times tonight. But first, he wanted to hear her scream as she came on his tongue.

****

Piper lie on her back with her arms at her sides, sucking in as much oxygen as she could get. They'd used up the last three condoms she'd had buried in her nightstand. And it was well after midnight. Both of them were covered in a sheen of sweat, her heart felt like it would burst through her ribs, and her bed was officially a mess. She wasn't even sure where the pillows or blankets had fallen.

For someone who had almost zero experience in the bedroom, Luke sure knew how to push all of her buttons. She'd lost count of how many times she'd orgasmed in the last few hours, but it seemed like Luke had made it his personal mission to see how many times he could get her to cry out his name.

He was pretty dang sexy when he came. He released this guttural, throaty grunting sound every time and it made Piper's insides turn to goo.

For the first time in her life, she'd felt like she was living out the scenes of one of those romance novels she loved so much. She'd always wondered where the authors had gotten their ideas for those scenes. Now she knew. They must have mind blowing sex. Because right now, Piper felt like she could use her night for the hottest book ever. That is, if she'd been a writer.

Shame she wasn't one to kiss and tell because she could give Nova so much fodder for her next naughty book.

Luke was lying on his stomach, his face turned to the side, his arms folded under his face.

"Maybe that was why I waited so long," he said so softly she almost didn't hear him.

"What?" She turned on her side to face him.

"I was just thinking." One shoulder moved like he was trying to shrug in his awkward position.

For a second, she could've sworn he was going to mark her. He'd been taking her from behind, had bent over her back, and she'd felt his teeth lightly graze the back of her neck. That was where feline Shifters marked their female mates. Males didn't get marked. They didn't need to. The females were claimed. The males were allowed to have as many females as they could claim. Anything to produce more cubs for the Prides.

Pushing those thoughts aside so they wouldn't ruin this dreamy moment, Piper folded her hands under her cheek and waited for Luke to finish his thought.

"I don't know. I had sex at seventeen. I thought I loved her. Then, her parents were trying to force us to pair up and I was already terrified of hurting her or anyone else. I'd barely even hung out with her other than to sneak off and make out. And eventually screw around. I always thought the reason I stopped sleeping with anyone after that was the fear of forming a bond with a female. But maybe my bear knew you were coming. Maybe he knew no one would ever compare to this, to you, to what we just did."

Her heart was back to racing but for a different reason now and the back of her eyes burned with unshed tears. She couldn't let them fall, couldn't let him think he'd upset her.

His eyes rolled up to hers and focused on her. "I didn't want a mate. But I want you, Piper."

"I want you, too," she whispered and wiggled a little closer. He rolled onto his side and opened his arms, welcoming her even closer until her backside was pressed against his front, his arms wrapped around her, holding her, shielding her, protecting her.

"Will you stay with me tonight?" she whispered into the dark night.

"I need to keep a watch out for trouble," he said, his breath warm on his neck as he buried his face in her hair.

"You can do that in here. Just… stay with me tonight. Get some sleep. Your people made my house an impenetrable fortress. No one will get in without one of us hearing them." She was smiling and she hoped that came across in her voice.

His body shook a little as he chuckled. "They did put a shit load of locks on your place. They'll have to crash through the front window to get in."

"See? We'll hear that. I mean, you might have to fight someone naked. And I can Shift and help. I might be small, but my cougar has claws and teeth, just like those jerks."

"Assholes."

"What?"

"They're assholes. Say assholes."

Piper's cheeks instantly heated. He wanted her to cuss? The words never sounded right coming from her mouth, even when she tried to sound tough. "Assholes," she said softly and then buried her face in the crook of his arm.

"There's my little warrior," he said with another chuckle.

They're laughter faded as did their conversation. They both had to work in the morning, Luke much earlier than Piper. But at least they'd have a few more hours together before they had to go their separate ways.

Callie was supposed to come hang out with her at the library tomorrow. She was going to pretend to do a research assignment so it wouldn't look weird that she was there all day. Micah hadn't been happy about that, but no one expected tiny Callie to fight anyone off. She was just an extra alarm system, a way to get a hold of the cavalry if Barrett or Andrew or anyone else showed up. She'd help Piper buy some time, help hold them off until Luke or someone else could get there.

She still hated the idea that Luke and all his people were putting themselves out for her. But…she was thankful for it. She'd just resigned herself to a daily fight until her mind splintered and she went along with whatever her parents demanded of her.

Would they back off now that she'd found someone? If Luke marked her, would they finally leave her alone to live her life the way she wanted? Sure, he was a bear, not a cougar, but it was a mate, a way to give her cubs some day in the future.

Wait. Did Luke want cubs? She'd always thought she didn't, but now, with Luke in her life, she was beginning to see her future a whole different way. He'd been resistant to mating because he feared he'd be abusive like his dad. He was probably just as scared of doing that to his own child. Piper had zero doubt Luke would be a good mate and a good father. No matter how much he doubted himself, she knew in her heart he'd spend his life doting on his family and giving them things he'd never had…like love.

Chapter Nine

Piper couldn't wipe the smile off her face as she listened to Luke using her shower. Luckily for them both, she had a supply of extra toothbrushes under the vanity. For once, her weird quirks worked in her favor.

The sound of him doing his mundane morning routine was so domestic and comfortable. Instead of the awkwardness of the morning after the first night of sex, she was energized and ready for a new day. The only thing that could've made it better was if he'd marked her. And she'd marked him.

In a short couple of months, she'd gone from resisting a future with a mate to wanting nothing more than having Luke in her bed every night. And who knew? Maybe it would get her parents to leave her alone. Maybe they could go back to pretending she no longer existed, the way they did before she hit puberty.

Yeah, right. She'd never had that kind of luck.

"What time do you go in to work?" Luke asked, stepping into the hallway wearing nothing but the jeans he'd worn over the night before.

Everything about this man oozed sexuality and made her body warm at the mere sight. She wanted to make love to him again, but Luke had to leave. His workday started way earlier than Piper's and was far more physical. She already felt bad he'd be running on a major lack of sleep.

"I don't start until nine. Well, I like to get in around eight. I like the silence first thing in the morning and nothing but me and the books."

He nodded as he shoved the toothbrush back into his mouth, a tiny smile quirking up one smile of his mouth.

"I'm crazy about a book nerd," he muttered to himself as he stepped back into the bathroom.

Crazy about a book nerd. He'd just admitted he was crazy about her. Little butterflies stirred in her belly. She laid a hand over the spot to calm them. It didn't help. Those little suckers were buzzing like crazy, tickling her insides.

"You sick?" Luke asked as he stepped from the bathroom and flipped off the light.

Piper dropped her hand and swung it behind her back as if she could hide what she'd been doing.

"Nope. Fine." She smiled wide but Luke frowned like she was crazy. "Are you going to be late?"

He narrowed his eyes but there was a hint of a smile on those lips that had brought her so much pleasure last night.

"Trying to get rid of me?" He closed the space between them and dragged her closer with his hands tight on her hips. Luke bent at the waist and stole a kiss, lingering long enough to urge Piper's body to push herself closer as if it was on autopilot.

When Luke pulled away, there was a crooked, sexy, yet slightly cocky grin on his face.

"Yeah. I'm going to be late. But those fuckers are always late. They can wait for me for once."

He slapped her on the ass, earning a squeal from Piper, then stepped past her to pluck his shirt from the couch. Even the act of redressing was sexy on Luke. Everything he did was sexy, at least to Piper.

Was this what falling in love felt like? Was it even possible to fall so quickly? They had weeks in each other's presence, but had really only spent hours together. First, the grocery shopping trip. Then the bar. And the run in the woods. And finally, they're time together last night. It seemed too fast. But…they weren't human. They didn't follow the same laws and love rules that humans did. Their animals tended to know long before their human sides when they'd found their soul's mate.

She should be happy to have found hers. Even if she'd been reluctant for so long.

So why did she feel terrified as she watched him pull the door closed behind him with a parting wink? It was like, for the first time in her life, she felt like she truly had something to lose.

And that something was sauntering to his truck with a swagger she'd only ever read about in books.

Standing in the doorway, she raised her hand and smiled when Luke waved goodbye, then waited until he was out of sight before she shut the door and turned to look at her room. She had two hours before she would head to the library. That was plenty of time to straighten up and shower before heading into House Springs.

Piper alternated between humming happily under her breath as she rearranged the pillows on her couch until they were lined up the way they were supposed to be, to frowning and fretting as she cleaned the already clean kitchen. She vacuumed her carpet with a little too much force but she couldn't get her brain and heart to agree on anything this morning.

She should be happy. She'd found someone who'd accepted her the way she was, who wanted her even if she was too skinny, who wanted nothing but what was best for her. Yet, the fear of having that happiness ripped to shreds was always right there on the surface. It wouldn't be past her Pride to attack Luke for no reason other than to hurt Piper. They would kill him, and she'd be right back to where she'd started.

She didn't need her cougar to call her a liar; she knew her life would never be the same if she lost Luke.

Once Piper was secure with her house's cleanliness, she showered and dressed. Only, this time, she skipped her usual cardigan and donned one of the sweaters Nova had bought her. It was still conservative enough that she didn't feel like she was advertising her body, begging other males to look at her, begging for attention from men who'd try to claim her. Yet, it was still far enough outside of her comfort zone that she felt like she'd accomplished a pretty big feat.

One big feat. That was all she could handle for the day. So she pulled on her slacks and slid her feet into a pair of simple flats that went well with the deep purple sweater. Hair dried and smoothed, makeup applied and she was ready for work.

She'd forgotten to ask whether Callie would meet her at home or at work. Honestly, she still felt a little bad about making someone she'd just met spend all day at the library with her. Most people didn't get excited by the smell of books like Piper did. That smell was better than cookies baking or flowers or even the most expensive perfume. Even better than her arsenal of cleaning products she kept under the kitchen sink. Those she didn't organize by alphabet. They were arranged by purpose and room, instead.

Callie wasn't outside Piper's house when she left, but she was standing outside the front doors of the library when Piper pulled into the parking lot.

Raising her hand, she grinned wide at the excited look on Callie's face.

"Hey," Callie said softly when Piper was close enough. "Thanks for getting me out of the house. I was going stir crazy."

"You sure hanging out here all day is anyone's idea of a fun time?" Piper said as she unlocked the front door and held it open for Callie to pass through. She relocked it behind them. She always locked herself in first thing in the morning. It wasn't until official opening time she was comfortable with the door being unlocked. Because, then, there'd be more witnesses in case Barrett decided to mess with her at work.

"Can I help you get set up for the day?" Callie asked, more excitement in her voice than should be there for someone who was stuck among row after row of fiction, nonfiction, collections of magazines and old newspapers, as well as some cake molds. Piper was always confounded by that part.

"Uh, sure," Piper said and pushed a cart toward her. "Do you remember the Dewey Decimal system?" Callie nodded, the grin still in place. "Well, just find the sections coinciding with the numbers on the spine of the books and put them back in order."

Callie nodded, her blonde hair swishing along her back, and headed toward the bookshelves with a bounce to her step.

"You're in a good mood," Piper said as she watched her.

"Mmmhmmm," Callie called back from somewhere deep in the library.

For a brief second, Piper almost asked why...then thought twice. She might've had a morning similar to Piper's evening. If that was why Callie was so chipper first thing in the morning, Piper didn't want the details. She might like to read about sex scenes, but she didn't want to hear her friends regale the gory details of their bedroom activities.

With the two of them working together, Piper's opening duties were done in half the time. So, they had about thirty minutes to kill before the other employees arrived.

Piper led Callie to a table near the center and carried two cups of cheap coffee from the carafe in the back, setting one in front of Callie.

"Thanks for coming today. I'm sorry if I screwed up your whole day." Piper sipped at the coffee and winced. Nothing like the stuff she made at home.

"Oh please. I've never had a job. I want to work, just..." She shrugged. "I still get a little jumpy sometimes. It's okay when my friends are around, like when we go to Moe's, but strangers?" With a shake of her head, she set the coffee down. "I'd make a fool of myself or let my eyes glow. So, I guess I should be thanking you for boring me today."

Piper chuckled softly. "Is that why you're in such a good mood? Or are you generally a bubbly morning person?"

Piper wasn't a morning person, but she wasn't a night owl either. Her best hours were the middle of the day when her mind and hands were busy at work and there were people who needed answers from her.

"No. Not a morning person," she giggled and lifted her cup to her lips to hide the smile growing on her lips.

Well, now Piper was curious. Unless it was the sex thing, of course. "Are you going to tell me?"

Callie leaned forward even though there was no one else in the building who could hear her.

"We're friends, right?" Callie whispered.

Those butterflies were back in her belly. A man who cared for her and new friends. It was like overnight she'd gained a big family.

"Yeah. Yes. We're friends," Piper said a little too quickly and loudly.

"Okay. This is a secret. Like, you're the first person other than Micah to know."

"Are you pregnant?" Piper asked, her grin growing as excitement built in her chest.

"Not yet. But we're officially trying. We don't really want to tell anyone yet because then Luke will get all weird about me hanging around and demand I stay home."

And that statement erased the smile from Piper's face. "What? Why would he do that? Why would he keep you from hanging out with me if you're trying to get pregnant?"

"It's not the trying part. And it's not that he wouldn't want me to hang out with you. I just couldn't be on 'guard duty'," she said, forming air quotes with her fingers around the words as she rolled her eyes. "He's super protective of us. Of all of us. Especially the women. And the second he finds out I'm knocked up he'll want me as far away from anything that he considers dangerous."

Super protective. Especially of the women. And Piper now knew why. But that wasn't her story to tell. If Luke had felt it necessary to hide that from the people he was closest to she had no intention of telling his secret.

"That's really great, Callie," Piper said, reaching out and touching Callie's forearm. It was awkward after going so many years with zero affection, but it felt natural. Everything with Luke and his people felt natural, like the life she'd lived before them had been faked and forced and this was where she was meant to be.

The rest of the day went by with zero drama and nothing nearly as excited as finding out not only that Callie was trying for a family, but that she'd told Piper before anyone else in her Pack. She'd confided in her. They really were friends. Or at least they were getting there.

Part of Piper, this sort childish side kind of wished her brother or mother or father would see her out with the Clan and Pack. She wanted them to see that they were wrong, that she wasn't undesirable and unlovable. She wanted them to see how happy she was, how happy these people made her. But that wasn't a good idea. They weren't the kind of people who would back down easily. And she felt guilty enough about everything they were already doing for her; she didn't want to be responsible for any of them getting into a fight or getting hurt...or worse.

"Thanks for hanging out," Piper told Callie as they walked side by side to their cars.

"Are you kidding? I've actually never officially been to a library. I had no idea there was so much in those places." When they were far enough away from any humans, Callie leaned her head closer. "You don't lose control of your animal at work?"

Piper shrugged and shook her head. "Nope. Never have. Maybe I should knock on wood or something before I get all cocky."

Callie laughed. The women said their goodbyes and headed to their own homes. Piper's mind was already there. Was Luke at her house yet? Or was someone else coming to hang out until he was ready for his nightly routine?

More importantly, would he stay the night with her in her bed again?

She'd never been with a virgin, other than when she was one, too. He wasn't technically a virgin, but it had been long ago enough that he'd been nervous. She'd originally thought his trembling was from desire or even him fighting his bear. She'd had no idea at first it was from nerves.

Piper had taken control of the situation to take the pressure off him. But after that first time, he'd been the one who'd taken control. He'd been nervous he wouldn't please her…and oh how wrong he'd been. She was sure she was still glowing hours later.

Luke wasn't there when she pulled into her driveway. It was Emory and Eli. Piper really liked the petite woman. Probably because they were so close to the same size. A few of the women in Big River were short like her; that made her less self-conscious about her height. But where they were as short and thin as her, they all had curves and breasts…unlike Piper.

But that didn't matter to Luke. He sure appeared to enjoy her small chest last night.

A smile stretched across her face as she pushed from her car and met Emory and Eli on her front porch. Eli was so much bigger than his mate. Almost twice her size. The girls had told her about Luke feeling like a failure at protecting Emory from an attack in Eli's former Pride. Luke had told Piper that Eli was a lion. Their entire group was comprised of a mixture of Shifter species. And for some reason, she had this excited feeling when she thought about the different babies that would be born over the years.

There could be cubs of different kinds, pups, all kinds of different Shifter children.

"You look happy," Emory said, stepping off the stairs and wrapping her arms around Piper's shoulders. She'd been hugged more in the last few days than she ever had in her life. It was something she'd have to get used to if she wanted to stay in Luke's life. Really, though…she kind of liked it. She'd never really known what she'd been missing until this big, crazy, loud group came crashing into her life.

"I am," Piper said as she stepped out of Emory's arms. "Thanks for coming over."

"Any problems today?" Eli asked, his eyes scanning Piper's property and narrowing to see as far into the trees as his human eyes would let him.

"Nope. Boring day. It was glorious."

Piper unlocked the door and jumped at the loud screeching sound coming from beside the door.

"What the hell?" she yelled, slapping her hands over her ears.

Eli stepped beside her and his fingers pushed a couple of numbers until the screeching stopped with one final beep.

"Luke had someone install an alarm system with a panic button. Apparently, he had it set to panic constantly," Eli said in his deep voice.

"What? When did he do that?"

"Today. While you were at work," Emory said, leaning forward to check out the box attached to the wall.

Piper's wide eyes went from the alarm, to Emory, up to Eli, then back to the alarm. "How did he even get in here?"

"They changed your locks yesterday and he has a key. You didn't notice your key was different?" Emory said, nodding down to the keyring in her hand with three keys. Her house, her car, and the library. That was all she had on the simple, metal keyring.

Pulling the key to her house free from the others, she realized it did look slightly different, but not enough for her to have noticed when she shoved it into the doorknob. "Huh."

"You're not mad?" Emory asked.

Piper shrugged. "I guess not. I mean, it's probably a good thing they changed my locks because my brother used to let himself in whenever he wanted."

"I mean, you're not mad that he made a key without telling you and had someone come into your house when you weren't home and install an alarm system?"

Emory's brow was raised and she tilted her head a little as she waited for Piper to answer.

Was she mad about it?

No. She wasn't. She'd grown used to Barrett's intrusions. And this was nothing like that. These people didn't bully their way into her life, didn't demand anything from her. They just wanted what was best for her. They wanted to keep her safe.

And honestly, Piper didn't mind Luke having a key to her house. It was one more step in growing this thing between them. He could let himself in at night instead of roaming the woods in his bear form and then trudge through the day exhausted. Even if he fell asleep and someone made it onto her property unnoticed, they couldn't get into the house without the alarm blaring and waking up both Piper and Luke. Unless several members of her Pride attacked at once, Luke and Piper could Shift and kick some butt. Well...Luke could. Piper could just help hold someone off him until he was ready to go all feral bear on the next guy.

They could be one bad *a* team. Yep. Even in her own head cussing would make her uneasy.

"No. I'm not mad. It's kind of sweet, even if a tad on the creepy side. But out of the people who've let themselves in my house, Luke is that last person I'd be upset about."

"Other people let themselves into your house? I thought you were kind of a loner," Emory said, making herself at home and heading straight for the fridge. "Got anything to eat?"

"Oh! I can make you something. Luke never lets me cook for him."

Emory's head popped over the top of the open fridge door. "Can you cook?" she asked with one brow raised.

"Yep. That's actually something I'm pretty good at." And her good mood got even better. Finally! She'd been trying to get Luke to let her feed him for a couple of days now. It was boring to cook for herself, so she usually cooked a couple times a week, then ate the leftovers the rest of the days.

Piper asked Emory and Eli what they wanted to eat, but they were both open to anything. Well, *Emory* was up to anything. Eli just shrugged and jerked his head toward Emory as if deferring the decision to his mate.

So, since she didn't have any specific requests, she went to work making her favorite baked chicken recipe. It was crispy like fried chicken, only without all the grease and mess. By the time she was done and making a side salad, her phone chirped indicating a text. Emory gave herself permission to read the message.

"Luke said he'll be over in about an hour. Has some errands."

Piper looked over her shoulder and smiled. "Thanks." Good mood continuing to grow.

"You know…maybe I shouldn't be reading your texts. That would've grossed me out if it'd been something dirty," Emory said as she set Piper's phone on the counter beside where she was working.

Cheeks flaming, Piper lowered her head and tried to focus on the food she was preparing instead of wondering if Luke would ever send her a sexy text.

"Hope you're not trying to pretend you two have never done it because I can smell Luke all over this place. And all over you," Emory said, a smile in her voice.

After a few deep breaths, Piper got her heart rate under control and prayed her cheeks weren't the color of flamingoes as she carried the food to the table and went back to the kitchen for the plates. She made extra so Luke would have something when he got there. It was dang time he tasted her cooking.

"Oh!" Emory said, standing in front of the couch and looking outside. "It's snowing. Heyyy! Maybe we'll get lucky and have a white Christmas."

Piper frowned. Christmas was only a couple of weeks away. She'd never experienced all that stuff they showed on commercials, never experienced huddling around a fire with her family while they sipped hot chocolate or went looking at lights with the carols playing on the radio. Shoot. She'd never even had a tree growing up. To her, December was just another month she had to get through. Another thirty-one days she had to survive without being forced into anything.

And then the new year came and she counted it as another year of success. But Emory appeared more than excited about the snow coming so close to the twenty-fifth. Was her house exploding with red and green? Did she have lights attached to the front of her place?

That great mood Piper had been in began to wane until a case of melancholy settled over her. She'd never grieved for the loss of the holidays. How could she grieve something she'd never experienced? But now she wished she could get as excited as Emory was. Now she wished...

"Hey Emory?" Piper asked as she sat down at the table. Emory and Eli were already piling their plates with several legs and breasts and drowning their salad in dressing.

"'Sup?" Emory replied without looking up from her food.

"Would you go Christmas shopping with me? I have no idea how to do it. I've never bought a gift for anyone or wrapped one before."

Emory's hand froze halfway to her mouth.

"What?"

"Would you go Christmas shopping with me? I want to get something for Luke."

"No. I mean...you've never bought a gift before?"

Eli cleared his throat and then Emory jumped slightly as if her mate had kicked her under the table.

"N-no," Piper said, suddenly regretting asking. She hated the look Emory was giving her, a mixture of pity and confusion.

"Of course, I'll go with you. But if I were you, I'd ask Nova, too. If she finds out we went shopping without her she'll pout for weeks."

"Everyone can come," Piper said, her mood rising again. Rollercoaster emotions. But hey, it was better than the numbness she'd been shrouded in for the last ten years.

****

"You know I'm close to slapping the shit out of you, right?" Luke told Reed as he wandered up and down the aisles of Christmas trees. It was cold and snowing tonight and Luke was ready to just grab a tree and go. In fact, he'd been content buying a plastic, pre-lit one and taking it to Piper's.

But Reed, Lola, and Nova had insisted he get her a real one for her first Christmas. And, no matter how much he protested, they demanded they come along to buy the decorations and help him put everything up. The wolves were always inviting themselves anywhere they damn well pleased.

"Stop being pissy. You said this was her first Christmas. We gotta do this shit right," Reed said as he inspected the fiftieth tree. "This one. This one is perfect."

"You sure it's not too tall?" Lola said, craning her neck to see the top.

"It should fit. What about the width? How big is her place, Luke?" Nova said, stretching her arms wide and wrapping them as far as she could around the pine.

"It'll fit," Luke said, rubbing the back of his neck.

The back of his truck was filled with bags of ornaments, stockings, fuzzy shit to wrap around the tree, lights, and even a fucking inflatable Santa for Piper's front yard. He'd wanted to give her a good Christmas, not make her house a replica of the North Pole.

"So? Are you going to wait until she's at work and surprise her?" Lola asked as Reed loaded the tree into the back of his own truck since nothing else would fit in Luke's.

"I work the same time she does," Luke said, forcing a softer look on his face. "She'll still be surprised."

"Oh! I know! We can be quiet and set up outside first. That way, she'll still be surprised. Want me to text Emory and warn her so Eli doesn't go all Alpha lion on us?"

With a heavy sigh, Luke nodded and closed his eyes. This was turning into so much more than he'd planned. He'd only meant to get her a tree, maybe one of those pre-lit four-foot trees. But his dumb ass mentioned it to Reed who brought his mate who brought along money bags herself. Luke had had to let Nova pay for a box of ornaments to get her to stop whining.

Nova had her phone in her hand tapping out a message as she walked over to the passenger side of Luke's truck. Lucky him, he got the nosiest member of Big River in his truck. It wasn't that she was a gossip; she was a writer and was always looking for new material for her dirty books. He did not want to star in her next one.

"Okay. I let Emory know we were coming and to keep Piper occupied for a bit while we set up outside." She got quiet for a second, then turned her upper body to look at him. "You think we need more lights for outside? How big is her place?"

"There's enough," Luke said, clenching his teeth to avoid snapping at her. He didn't mind being an asshole to the guys. But not the women. Never the women. No matter how much they chattered on beside him or how much more nervous they made him about this gesture.

Was he getting ahead of himself? He'd been adamant his whole life about avoiding the mating bond. But he couldn't see himself living without Piper. She was everything he'd ever wanted. Which, of course, scared the shit out of him even more than anything ever had in his life.

Five minutes. Luke would pull his truck onto Piper's driveway in five minutes. They'd already discussed turning off their headlights and parking closer to the road in hopes Piper wouldn't hear their vehicles.

By the time Luke put his car in park and pushed from his seat, his stomach was in knots. He'd never done anything like this for someone, had never sought out ways to simply see someone smile. He wanted Piper happy. He wanted to give her something she'd never had. He wanted to see her eyes light up as she checked out all the colors and glowing lights.

The four of them pulled everything out of the bags before heading up to the house; Nova said the crinkling of the plastic would be another alert to Piper's sensitive Shifter ears. So, as quickly and quietly as they could, they hung lights and a wreath, set up a big, plastic manger scene, and plugged in the inflatable Santa. There was loud music coming from inside the house as if they were watching an action flick on the loudest possible level. *Good thinking, Em.*

As soon as they were done with the outside, Luke slipped his newly made key into the lock, knocked three times, then pushed inside, the Christmas tree behind him as Reed carried the end.

"Hey," he said as he stepped in.

Piper slowly stood, her eyes going from Luke's face, to the tree he was carrying, then back up.

"What is this?"

"A Christmas tree," Luke said with a shrug, suddenly feeling sheepish.

"For me?" Her voice was so soft, her eyes wide, her cheeks slowly flushing a soft pink.

"All of it's for you, girlie," Nova said as she stepped in behind Luke with the bags of ornaments and other decorations.

Piper watched silently as they set up the tree, wrapped the lights, set out a few other things around the house like candles, and then turned to Piper expectantly.

Luke lifted his hand, offering her the first box of ornaments. They were simple glass balls in various colors. If she liked the holiday, he'd take her every year after to pick out a new one for the tree.

And then he realized he was already thinking of their future instead of dwelling on the uncertainty and fear he'd originally been feeling.

Piper glanced down at the ornaments then up to Luke.

"You should hang the first one," he said. Shit. Maybe this was opening wounds she'd rather ignore. He'd thought she would like all this, would like her first Christmas tree and all that crap.

Her hands were shaking as she took the box from him, opened it, then walked over to the tall, wide tree Reed set inside a stand right in front of her picture window. Lola was already in the kitchen getting water for the big thing.

After Piper hung a single ornament, she stepped back and stared at it. When she turned to look at Luke, her eyes were glassy with unshed tears, but her smile was wide and full of joy.

"I have a Christmas tree," she said a little louder then clapped her hands together once and held them in front of her chest. "Thank you so much!"

The room was suddenly alive as everyone crowded Piper and helped her decorate the tree with everything else. Once they were done, her house looked like one of those commercials, complete with carols playing on the radio hanging under a cabinet in Piper's kitchen.

"I can't believe I'm going to have a Christmas!" Piper breathed out, standing in the middle of her living room and making slow circles to look at everything.

"There's more!" Nova exclaimed, then made a face at Luke when he frowned at her. "Sorry. I'm just so freaking excited."

"More?" Piper asked in that sweet, feminine voice of hers.

"Come on," Luke said, holding his hand out to her.

He led her out into her yard so she could get a good look. They'd hung the lights along the front of the house and along the deck. The Santa was whirring softly, the manger scene was lit up, and the wreath on her door had twinkly lights.

Tears were back in Piper's eyes as they slowly assessed her house. She turned to Emory and laughed. "That's why you wanted to watch that god awful movie."

"Hey! I saw what you were watching. *Die Hard* is a Christmas necessity," Reed said as if offended.

"Is it too much?" Luke asked when she turned to him.

"No way! This is perfect. Thank you so much!"

"They helped," Luke said, twitching his head in the direction of their audience.

"But it was his idea," Lola said.

And then Piper was stepping into his body and wrapping her arms around his waist, her cheek resting against his chest. She sighed heavily, her body expanding and shrinking against him as he held her tight.

"We're going to head home. Glad you like it, girlie," Nova said as they all quietly made their way to their vehicles and left Piper and Luke embracing on the front porch.

The wind had picked up and it was getting colder as icy flakes brushed across the faces and landed in their hair to melt, but he couldn't make himself pull away from her and guide her inside. He wanted to stay right there in her arms for as long as he could. Because the second they pulled apart, it was like a reminder that there was a world outside their little bubble.

Chapter Ten

Piper's heart was full. Her chest felt like it would explode with all the emotions she was trying to hold in. Luke had given her something she'd never had. He'd remembered their conversation about not having a Christmas and gone out of his way to make it special for her. She had a feeling a lot of the stuff other than the tree was Nova's idea or even Lola's, but that was fine.

He'd given her more than he could ever realize.

They lie in her bed, naked, tangled in each other's arms as the sweat dried on their skin and their breathing echoed in the dark room. They'd made love twice since his friends had left. Her friends. *Their* friends. She had friends now. She had people who cared about her and wanted her safe and happy.

"Piper," Luke said, his voice deep and growly and soft.

"Yeah?" she breathed out against his chest as her cheek rested on his shoulder.

His fingers tangled in her hair and his heart rate sped up again. He didn't say anything else.

Pushing up, she turned and rested her hand on his chest, propping her chin on the back of it so she could look into his face without sitting up. "What's wrong?"

"Nothing."

"Your heart is racing."

He lifted his head and cocked an eyebrow at her. "I did just make love to the most beautiful woman in the world. Twice." His grin was crooked as he winked and dropped his head back against the pillow.

"What did you want to say?"

He inhaled deep, his expanding chest raising her with the movement. "It's…it's too soon."

What was too soon? They're making love? Them? "What, Luke?"

He urged her off his chest, sat up against the headboard and turned her nightside lamp on. Piper squinted against the sudden onslaught and frowned at Luke.

"I don't want you to freak out."

"You're freaking me out by saying that. Just blurt it out before you think about it too much." What could he possibly have to say that he was too scared to tell her?

Luke pushed a hand through his already mussed hair and blew out a rush of air.

"I almost marked you," he whispered.

"I know." She'd felt the graze of his fangs when he'd barked out his last release.

"I need to mark you."

"I know." She felt the same way.

He glanced down at her, away, then back down at her again. "That doesn't freak you out?"

She shrugged up her shoulders, tugged the sheet up higher so she was covered. Not that Luke hadn't officially seen every inch of her body already. "I guess it should. But it doesn't."

Luke dragged a rough hand down his face with a groan. "I don't know why I'm still fighting it."

"I do. Even Shifters suffer from PTSD. I think if it'd been anyone but you, I'd be running away screaming." She giggled but Luke didn't return the smile. She turned so she was facing him instead of sitting up beside him. "Will you ever hurt me? Hit me? Pull my hair?"

"Absolutely not."

"And I believe you. One hundred percent. I trust you more than I've ever trusted anyone in my life, Luke. You've given me so much in such a short time. I have friends now. A family. People who actually care about something other than what's between my legs."

His eyes dropped to where the sheet was covering her nudity and a light flared up behind his irises before fading. No doubt he was thinking about all the ways they'd explored each other's bodies over the last two hours. For someone with no experience in the bedroom he sure made love like a pro.

He blinked rapidly and Piper realized his eyes were glassy. He was holding back tears. Had she said something to hurt him? Had she brought up memories he'd shoved deep down?

"I love you, Piper," he whispered, his lips barely moving. "I've loved you for a while now. Maybe since that first day. I just didn't know what it felt like. Didn't know what it was. But…I love you. So much."

Piper's lips popped open in surprise. He'd been holding back emotion over how he felt about her.

"I love you, too," she whispered back. "I want you to mark me. Like my kind do. And then I want you to mark me like a bear." Females didn't mark their mates, not in Prides. But Piper had every intention of leaving hers on Luke before the sun rose. When morning came, she wanted the whole world to know they belonged to each other.

Luke lifted his arms and she immediately moved closer, her breasts pressed against his hard chest. She let the sheet fall and threw a leg over his lap, straddling him and his already growing erection. Their lips met with so much want, hunger, and love.

There was no fanfare, no foreplay. Piper reached between their bodies and lined the head of hardness against her opening and slid down inch by inch, taking him in slowly and giving her body time to readjust to his size.

Luke moaned against her lips, sending a thrilling sensation throughout her body until she shivered against him. His arms tightened around her, holding her in place for a moment, only a moment. And then his hips began to move, pushing up, pushing himself deep inside of Piper's warmth.

****

Being with Piper was everything he could've dreamed and nothing he'd known was possible. She was so warm, so tight and wet for him again. He could've continued to push into her all night, but she hadn't grabbed a condom this time.

Pulling his lips from hers, he said, "Protection," and chuckled deep when she groaned. She didn't want to lift off of him, didn't want him to leave her tightness.

Fine. He wouldn't. Lifting onto his knees with her still wrapped around his cock, Luke scooted until he could reach her nightstand and the new supply of rubbers he'd bought before meeting up with the wolves from Big River. Even with his stealthy maneuvers, he still had to pull from her long enough to put the damn condom on.

But Piper made rolling the latex over his length the most erotic fucking thing of his life. By the time she was pinching the tip of the reservoir, he was damned near cross eyed.

He couldn't wait another second. He was achy and shaking with need. Lifting Piper, he speared her with his cock hard and fast, pulling a scream from her lips as she threw her head back. Waiting long enough to ensure himself he hadn't hurt her, he began to lift her the same time he pulled his hips back, then pulled her back down to meet his thrusts. They were panting, grunting, moaning, their sounds mixing with the sound of flesh hitting flesh.

His gums throbbed as his fangs dropped, the need to mark her taking over every other instinct. She wanted him to mark her like a bear, but also like her people. He was more than happy to oblige.

But before Luke could open his mouth and gently latch onto the spot where her shoulder met her neck, Piper leaned forward and bit him. She moaned as her body tightened around him. He had to pull up every unsexy image he could to hold back. She was milking him, spasming around him and the feeling of her lips pressed against his shoulder, her teeth deep in his flesh pushed him too far.

The second he could tell Piper was coming down from her orgasm and had pulled her fangs from his shoulder, Luke pulled from her, turned her onto her stomach, and pulled her ass up into the air. She squealed in surprise.

And then he knelt behind her and admired the sight of the most perfect round and perky ass he'd ever seen in his life. With a hand wrapped around his cock, he guided himself back into her, then grabbed her hips with both hands. They were right back to hard and fast. He'd never known what he'd like when and if he finally had sex again. And maybe he still didn't know. But right now, in this moment, he needed everything Piper could give him.

As he felt his balls tighten and the first tingles ripple through his body, Luke leaned over Piper's back, lifted her hair from her neck, and slowly sunk his fangs into the flesh there. She moaned, her insides tightening again as the mark pushed her toward another release. How many had she had so far? He hadn't bothered to count, but the fact she was having a second so soon gave him a rush of manly pride. He'd done that. He'd make his mate feel good.

His mate. His. She was his. And he was hers. They'd sealed the deal, were letting the world know who they belonged to. After this night, there would be a change to Piper's blood. Any Shifter within a certain distance would know she was mated. Not just claimed by some asshole, but bonded to her true mate. The one person the universe had chosen for her. For him.

He was the luckiest fucker in history.

Breath coming in deep pants, Luke gently pulled from Piper and helped her onto her back, then disposed of the condom. He needed a shower, but he'd much rather snuggle up beside Piper. There might've been a change to her blood, but something had changed inside of him, too. He was still protective and terrified of losing her; those sensations only became stronger. There was more, though. He felt…lighter. As if he could take on the world without batting an eye. All those memories, all those sounds he was constantly swallowing back and trying to drown out seemed quieter. Piper's existence had healed a broken part of him, glued those cracks back together, made him feel whole for the first time in his life.

Rolling onto his side, Luke pulled Piper until she was once again lying on his chest, her arm thrown over his waist, her leg over his thighs. She yawned so big her jaw popped and then she giggled.

"I don't think I've ever been so tired and not been crabby about it. Blissful exhaustion," she murmured, her breath cooling the sheen of sweat drying on his chest.

She sighed in contentment and, within minutes, her body relaxed and her breathing became slow and steady. She'd fallen asleep fast. If only his brain would shut down to rest that easily.

She should rest easily, though. Between himself, his Clan, and the wolf Pack, they had Piper covered. Her locks were reinforced, he'd had an alarm installed by the Alpha of Lola and Reed's former Pack, and there was always someone watching over her, providing her with back up, watching her back when she was busy at work.

Would her family back off now that she was mated? That was what they'd wanted all this time, after all. He might not be a cougar or even an Alpha, but he'd love their daughter and protect her. Shit. Those assholes didn't care about either of those things. Otherwise, they wouldn't approve of her piece of shit brother abusing her every chance he got.

Had he attempted to contact her recently? It'd only been a few days since Piper had had a twenty-four-hour shadow; had he noticed yet? Luke could see that prick, Barrett, threatening her, warning her to get rid of Luke and the others. But his mate was strong, stronger than her brother, or mother, or father, or any other asshole in her Pride gave her credit for. Stronger than any of them could ever dream of being.

A plan began to develop in Luke's head as sleep began to drag him under. He'd hunt down Barrett, let him know Piper was claimed and properly mated by her true mate. That she was happy. He'd threaten him, pass along a message to their parents that she was officially off the market.

And then Luke and Piper could live happily ever after.

If only things ever worked out that easily.

Luke was up and in the shower before Piper's eyes opened. He was as quiet as possible, making sure to start her coffee and plug in her tree before she wandered out of her room. He wanted her to have the same joy waking that she'd had when she spotted the tree last night.

She was still in bed by the time Luke was clean and dry. This time, though, he'd had enough foresight to bring along a change of clothes. Shame he couldn't talk her into moving into his cabin with him. For one thing, she truly loved her quaint little house. Two, it was a little soon to be talking about living situations, even if they both knew there was no way they could ever part, not now that they carried each other's marks.

And three…he hadn't even invited her to his house yet. What would she think of his bachelor pad? It wasn't messy, per se, but it sure as fuck wasn't as clean and girly as her place. Where her home smelled sweet and so much like her, his house smelled like him – sweat and dirt and fur. She'd probably have a damn stroke at how much laundry he had piled in his laundry room or how his movies and books were scattered around his living room, landing wherever he tossed them when he was done.

They were such opposites yet so much alike. They both carried scars, both physical and emotional, from their pasts. But she'd used those bad memories, those moments of horror to push herself to be different. She'd used cleaning and organizing as a way to show she was in control. Luke had turned out a little differently. He'd always been protective over women, but after he'd failed to keep Emory safe a year ago, he'd sunk into a dark place, only seeing moments of light when his friends and family found happiness or when the two little girls from Big River were born.

Speaking of babies – Had Shawnee told Colton yet? It was just a matter of time before she had to say something. And then the bear would be as reluctant to have Shawnee on guard duty as Luke already was.

A wave of excitement rolled over Luke. Colton had wanted a mate and a family for as long as Luke had known him. The bastard was going to be thrilled when he found out he was finally going to be a dad.

Luke hesitated in the doorway of Piper's room and watched her sleep. She was on her side, hugging his pillow to her chest, her lips slightly parted, her lashes dark against her pale skin. He'd never wanted to be a dad. Feared he'd turn out like his. But, just like his change of heart over mating Piper, he suddenly thought about how beautiful Piper would be with a belly rounded with his cub. And he didn't give a shit whether it was a cougar or bear cub, either.

Would she be open to something like that in the future? They were only in their mid-twenties; they had plenty of time to talk about it. And if she didn't want children, he'd be fine doting on her and the cubs and pups from his friends. Mainly Piper, though.

He wanted to see that same smile she had last night. There had to be even more she hadn't experienced. New Year's parties. Easter baskets. Fourth of July barbecues.

It was getting a little cold for their weekly cookouts, but with the fire pits and an extra layer, they should all be fine. For the first time, he was the one who wanted plan the damn get-together. He just wanted

Piper to experience everything. Even though Luke's dad had been a bastard, his mom had always made sure they had fun. There had been decorations for literally every single holiday, including coordinating salt-n-pepper shakers. His dad had broken some of them during a few of his rampages. But his mom would apply some makeup over the bruises and go find new ones.

Wow. Like he'd been hit upside the head, he realized how much Piper was like his mom. They both contained the same strength and resilience. He'd found someone identical to the only other woman he'd ever loved.

A smile bloomed slow and wide on his face as he padded softly to the side of the bed and lowered beside Piper. He leaned down and kissed her awake, leaving soft pecks on her cheek, forehead and temple.

"Hi," she whispered hoarsely. Turning onto her back, she stretched her arms over her head and made a little moan.

Moving quickly, Luke pulled the sheet up to her chin, covering those perky tits he'd had in his hands and mouth more than once last night. Between the sight of her body and that sound she was making he was rock hard and ready to lunge between her thighs.

He had to leave for work and she needed to get ready for hers. They'd both end up late if he acted on his desires.

"Coffee is going. I've got to head out to work." He leaned down and stole a kiss, but she pushed him away.

"Ew! I haven't brushed my teeth or showered yet." She pulled the sheet up until it covered her mouth. All Luke could do was chuckle.

For a few hours, she'd seemed to have forgotten about her incessant need for cleanliness. But he knew by the time he got back to her house tonight the bed would be made, the bathroom and kitchen spotless, and she'd have rearranged all her new decorations in a certain order only she'd understand.

And none of that bothered him in the least. He knew her behavior was borderline OCD if not full blown. But he also knew stress was a huge trigger for any form of mental disorders or behavioral twitches. Hopefully, in time, she'd become so relaxed in her new life she'd let some of the smaller things slide. And if not, it was part of who she was and he'd continued to love her the way she was.

"Call me later?" she asked, sitting up against the headboard and pulling the sheet and bedspread as if she were already making her bed while she was still lying in it.

"Absolutely." He kissed her forehead and held his hands up when she complained about her morning breath again. So fucking cute.

As he backed out of the room, bidding her goodbye one last time, he realized he'd found something that should've been on the gross factor cute. He found her obsessions endearing. And he realized he finally knew what being in love really meant. It meant accepting someone, flaws and all. It meant loving their scars and the demons they carried around inside of them. Hopefully, his demons weren't too scary for her to handle.

With a pep in his step he'd never had, Luke resisted the urge to whistle as he headed to his truck. He lifted his head and sniffed the air, making sure there was no one around waiting for him to leave so they could have Piper alone. Then he headed to the work site.

It was Peyton's turn to hang out with Piper at the library today. Since she'd been hired to teach the Shifter children after she'd had her animal forced into her and could no longer work with humans, her schedule was pretty flexible. There weren't all that many cubs, pups, or any other Shifter pups of school age locally. At least not until Big River's little girls grew up.

Of all the women who could hang with Piper, Luke preferred Peyton. Her animal was hostile, aggressive, downright violent when she thought anyone was after someone she saw as vulnerable or weak. No matter how much Big River taught Peyton about Shifter ways, her animal ruled the roost when it came to certain situations.

The rest of the guys were at the site by the time Luke pulled his truck next to theirs. Everyone had started driving their own vehicles as each male paired up with their mates. It was easier that way, whether simply to meet up with their mate or if they needed to run to her aid. Not that any of their women were damsels in distress. Even Piper and Shawnee, with their fucked up backgrounds, were strong women.

"How's Piper doing?" Carter asked, a grin wide on his face.

"Fine," Luke said as he passed.

"Did you hear the news?" Carter asked, that grin still in place.

Luke stopped walking and turned a frown on Carter. Then looked at Colton who was grinning just as wide. Maybe even wider, if that was at all possible. Shawnee had finally told him. But he sure as fuck wasn't going to tell either of them that he already knew.

"What's going on?"

"I'm going to be a daddy!" Colton said then busted into loud laughter. It sounded nervous and excited and full of the same kind of joy Piper had shown last night.

"Congrats, brother," Luke said, closing the space and pulling Colton into a bear hug. No pun intended. They smacked each other on the backs and Luke could've sworn he heard a sniffle come from Colton.

When they pulled apart, Colton was, indeed, wiping his eyes. "Shit. Don't tell Shawnee I cried," he said with a watery smile.

"How far along?" Luke asked. He had a vague idea since Shawnee had confided in him a week ago, but he wasn't sure.

"Only a month or so. We've got some time. She's already freaking out about whether she'll have to go on bedrest. I told her there's a chance it'll be a bear cub and she can keep working as long as she wants."

"That little woman carrying one of your big ass babies?" Luke said with a shake of his head as he headed toward the heavy equipment he'd be manning for the day. "Surprised she's not already on bedrest."

Luke smacked Colton on the back as he passed.

Three hours later and he was once again checking the time on his phone. He'd already sent Piper four text messages since he'd arrived. The first was making sure she got to work okay and that Peyton had made it. All was cool there. The rest were the same mushy shit he hated when his brothers all paired up. *Love you. Miss you. Can't wait to see you.* That kind of shit.

Christmas was only a week or so away. He wanted to get her a gift. Something to really make her smile. Of course, the one thing Luke really wanted to give Piper was freedom from her family. That was something she truly wanted more than anything.

As the day wore on, Luke began to build a plan in his head. He'd find a way to contact Barret or Piper's father and have a sit down with them, somewhere public, of course. He might be screwed up in the head, but he wasn't fucking stupid. Those kinds of people weren't honorable. If they thought Luke would be alone, they'd bring as many assholes as they could to take him out of the equation. And then Piper would be on her own again.

Not true. Piper was part of the family now. Even if he hadn't told his Clan brothers they'd marked each other last night, there was no doubt they could smell Piper all over him. And they'd definitely smell it in her blood the second they were close enough. She'd never be alone again. Even if something happened to Luke, his people, the Clan and the Pack, would take care of her, make sure she was safe, make sure no assholes fucked with her.

Peyton's really intense, Piper texted to him.

Luke felt his lips pull into a smile as he messaged her back.

"Yep. Dude's in love," Colton said from beside the Bobcat.

Finishing up his text, Luke slid his phone back into his pocket as he held up his middle finger, shoving it in Colton's face.

"Hey! There's nothing wrong with it. 'Bout damn time, though. My girl was worried about you."

"Yeah," Luke said as he went back to work. He knew very well how worried Shawnee had been. She'd never made it a secret that she wanted all the bears mated and growing families. In a way, she was getting what she wanted. Except Piper and Luke wouldn't be living within the territory, at least not anytime soon. He would never force her to leave the home she adored. He'd be just as happy cramming his big body in her house, as long as they were together.

Then again, they hadn't talked about cohabitating. Thoughts that it was a little soon to be talking about living together were once again circling each other. Even if Shifters tended to move fast by human standards.

It didn't matter if they technically lived together or not. Luke had been at her house for weeks before they'd uttered a single word to each other. And, even if she told him she didn't want him in her bed every night, he'd continue to keep her safe every night. He'd just do as he'd done before and roam the woods in his bear form.

Plans to warn Piper's family that she was off the market and mated began to play in his head again. He should tell Carter what he was thinking. That way, at least one other person would know what was going on and where he'd be in case anything went south. Not that he expected anyone to rush in and save the day. He just wanted to make sure they knew to keep an eye on Piper.

She was all that mattered. She was everything to Luke. Of course he loved his Clan family and the wolves. But the affection he'd felt for them all these years paled in comparison to the way he felt about Piper. He felt like one of those characters from one of Nova's romance books she was always writing. And he wasn't too proud to admit he'd read a couple of them.

"What did you get Piper for Christmas?" Colton asked as they finished their day and headed to their trucks.

"Nothing yet. There are two things I want to get her. Just not sure yet."

Carter set his hard hat on the hood of his truck. "What are you thinking?"

"Well…she likes clothes. I saw her when Nova brought all those sweaters over to her. I was thinking of asking one of the girls to go with me and get her some new stuff."

"She'd probably like that." Colton said, scratching at the stubble peppering his cheeks and jaw.

"What's the second one," Carter asked, his eyes narrowed as if he knew something was up and he wasn't going to like Luke's answer.

Hesitating, he pondered whether telling them everything was a good idea. But he'd already decided it was best for Piper and her safety. Even if he was killed, they would be able to find his body and give Piper closure. Eventually, she'd move on, find someone with a few less demons than Luke. Not that he was saying he didn't deserve her…even if he didn't. He only wanted to make sure she would be able to move on if this whole thing turned into a fucking disaster.

After Luke told Carter and Colton his plan, they nodded and seemed to be mulling over the information.

"You sure it's a good idea?" Carter asked.

"The only way I can think to get them off her ass."

"You going to tell Piper what you're doing?" Colton asked.

Luke rubbed the back of his neck. "Probably not. Not until after it's all said and done."

"She'll be pissed. Your little mate seems pretty strong. I think she could handle it if you're open with her. She might even want to go with you," Carter said, leaning against his truck with one elbow resting on the hood.

"No fucking way am I taking her anywhere near those mother fuckers. You should see her back. She's scarred from the middle of her back all the way down to her knees."

"Fuuuck," Carter growled out. "Who the fuck does something like that to their own kid?"

A long, low growl trickled nonstop out of Colton. He was thinking about his own kid on the way. Colton would never hurt anyone, especially his own child. And all of them, the Clan and the Pack and even their friends in the panther Pride, viewed anyone who would do shit like that as the lowest form of life.

"Tell us what you need us to do, man. We'll keep Piper safe. You know that. But we need to keep your hotheaded ass safe, too," Carter said, pushing from his truck and moving closer to Luke.

They came up with a plan to keep Piper out of the hands of her family's Pride, and hopefully, Luke, too. Only time would tell.

Now that that part had been ironed out, Luke had a scarier mission to plan: He had to go shopping for some women's clothes. The thought made him shudder.

Chapter Eleven

"Where's everyone else?" Piper asked as she climbed into Lola's car a couple days after Piper and Luke had marked each other. It was only Peyton and Lola. No Emory or Nova, or even Hollyn or June. She'd thought the women from her mate's Clan would want to join her on her first ever Christmas shopping trip.

Did they not approve of their pairing?

No way. All those women had been nothing but nice to her. And Hollyn was probably at work, just like Shawnee. That only left June and she'd been nothing but kind and accepting from the moment they'd met.

"Everyone's out running errands…or something," Lola said. Peyton glanced at her with one brow raised.

"You're a terrible liar," Peyton said, winking at Piper. "Luke recruited some help for your gift."

"He's getting me another gift?"

"He already gave you something?" Lola asked as she pulled into traffic.

"Uh, haven't you seen my house? He had to have spent a fortune on all that," Piper said, looking at Lola with wide eyes.

"You realize there's a good chance Nova bought most of that. That woman will use any excuse possible to buy things for people. She used to break into the Pack's houses and leave gifts. But it almost caused a fight between Gray and Micah. Or that's what Tristan told me."

"Told you or pantomimed?" Lola said.

"He might not talk much in front of you guys, but he talks in front of me," Peyton said with a sniff. She was trying hard to sound offended but there was a wistful smile on her face as she discussed her mate.

As Lola drove them into a more populated area with more stores than they had where they lived, Piper tried to think of what Luke could possibly get her. She had everything she could ever want. She had a new family who cared about her, a mate who loved her, a home, and her first Christmas tree. She felt like she was living inside one of those Hallmark movies they played during the holidays.

One store after another, Piper felt more and more lost. She had no idea what to get someone like Luke. What did one get their new mate? In all reality, they didn't know each other that well. She had no idea what his favorite color was or his favorite music or movies. All she knew was he was hers. And she was his.

She'd seen people wear those heart necklaces that had been split for each person to wear half. She'd always thought they were cute, but too girly for Luke. Those necklaces were better for sisters or best female friends. Not a big, scruffy Shifter.

"I don't know," Piper said as they walked out of yet another store. "What did you get your mates?" she asked the women beside her.

"I got Reed a streaming subscription. The boy loves his movies," Lola said with a smile.

"What about you?" Piper asked Peyton.

She shrugged up her shoulders. "I haven't gotten anything yet. I'm kind of lost this year, too. I was thinking something for his truck or maybe some new tools."

Her brows popped up. "Tools? You think Luke would like something like that?"

"I think these guys would be happy with anything we gave them. Stick from the yard? Best present ever," Peyton said with a wink.

An idea came to Piper's head as she listened. Climbing into the back seat of Lola's car, she pictured the look on Luke's face when she presented him with the only gift she could think of giving him. It would be way better than a set of screwdrivers or a new headlight for his truck. Besides, his truck was pretty worn out and rusty. He didn't appear to be one of those guys who'd treasure accessories for his vehicle.

"Could we go somewhere with bows and ribbon and stuff?"

"Like gift wrap?" Lola asked, glancing at Piper in the rear view. Piper nodded. "Everywhere has that stuff right now."

Lola pulled into another shopping center with rows of stores including a huge hardware store for Piper. The rest of the day went a lot more smoothly now that Piper had an idea of what she'd give Luke. She'd give him the only thing she could think he'd treasure…herself.

Peyton and Lola waved as they dropped Piper off at her house. It was the weekend so she wouldn't have to go in to the library for two more days. She never worked Saturdays. She liked her regular schedule, liked to know the exact days and hours she'd work every single week. But that also meant she had more time with Luke. He wasn't there when she was dropped off. Emory was sitting on the top step of Piper's porch with her mate, Eli, standing behind her, leaning forward onto the railing as they both watched Piper climb out of Lola's car.

"Hey," Piper said, raising her free hand as she carried her bag of bows closer.

Neither Emory nor Eli smiled, no greeting, no teasing.

"What's wrong?"

Emory jerked her head toward the house and followed Piper inside. Luke had a key to Piper's house, but he hadn't given one to any of his friends. For some reason, that made her trust Luke more. He wasn't taking advantage of her, wasn't taking over her house or her life.

Eli hovered near the front door as Piper set her bag on the kitchen table and her purse on the chair. Emory shifted her weight from one foot to the next, wringing her hands in front of her as she looked anywhere but at Piper.

Luke. This was about Luke. What else could possibly make her so nervous? Had he sent his people to dump her? No way. He was no coward. And Eli wouldn't look so tense and on the verge of Shifting if it was a simple relationship issue. And Emory's eyes were watery as she held back tears.

"What happened?"

Piper's legs trembled and her knees threatened to give out. Lowering onto the chair where she'd set her purse, she looked between Emory to Eli then back with wide eyes. Her heart raced in her chest, her breath came in ragged pulls. Trembling started in her hands and moved throughout her body, the anxiety of the current suspense threatening to either force her to pass out or Shift into her cougar.

"Tell me," Piper forced out through her closing throat.

"He met with your brother," Eli said, pushing away from the door and moving closer. "He wanted to give you your freedom. He wanted your Pride to know you'd found a mate. He wanted them to stay away from you."

"He wanted to protect you," Emory said, dropping to her knees in front of Piper, taking both hands in her own.

"Is he..." She couldn't form the words. Refused to believe something had happened to him.

"Last we heard, he's still alive. Your dad spoke with Gray and Carter. They want to make a trade," Eli said as a muscle ticked in his jaw.

"Me," Piper said. "They'll let Luke go if I go home."

"This is your home," Emory said. "Luke would kill us if we let you turn yourself over."

"They'll kill *him* if I don't," Piper said as her heart threatened to shatter into a thousand pieces.

She didn't want to return to the Donnell Pride. She didn't want to be paired and mated to Andrew. She didn't want to live with those people, didn't want to live without Luke. *Couldn't* live without Luke. She'd rather throw herself in front of a bus than live without the only male her heart had ever claimed.

And then Piper realized Eli had positioned himself directly in front of the door again. He'd backed away from Piper and leaned against the thick wood with his arms crossed over his chest.

Emory and Eli weren't there to keep her safe until Luke came home; they were there to keep her from leaving. They were there to keep her from turning herself over to her family.

"Where is everyone else?" Had Peyton and Lola known what was going on? If they did, they were the best actresses in history because they hadn't let on that anything was going on other than a shopping trip. "Is that why you and Nova and the rest of the women didn't go shopping with us?"

Emory's head wagged side to side. "We were all supposed to go shopping with him. He asked for our help in getting your Christmas present. But he never showed up. And then Carter got a call. And then Gray."

The room swam as Piper tried to make sense of what Emory was telling her. How could they possibly think she'd sit in her house while her mate was in the hands of the same people who'd tried to break her? She knew they wouldn't hesitate to kill him to get to her. They'd used him as another tool to crumble her resolve, tear her heart to shreds, break her spirit.

And it would work.

Without Luke, she was nothing.

"We can't do *nothing*," Piper said, shoving to her feet and rushing to the front door. Eli refused to move. "Eli! We have to help him! We have to go get him!"

"Carter's handling it," Eli said, that muscle in his jaw once again ticking. He was clenching his teeth, fighting his animal for control, trying to keep his skin when all he really wanted to do was rush over there and get his friend.

These people were loyal. They were fierce. No way would they *not* help Luke.

Piper turned to Emory to plead her case. If it had been Eli, Piper knew Emory would be the first one leading the charge. Any of the women would do that for their mates. They couldn't think she'd do any less.

"I want to go to Blackwater. I want to talk to Carter," Piper said.

Eli looked to Emory with a shrug. "We'll drive you."

They didn't trust her to not head to Donnell. She didn't blame them. There was a part of her that wanted to do exactly that. But it would be a suicide mission, so to speak. Her alone would do nothing to keep Luke safe. They'd still kill him, in front of her, so she'd know where the power lie.

Right in her parents' hands.

Grabbing her purse, Piper followed Eli through her front door with Emory right on her heels. She hadn't even bothered with the alarm. No one would be showing up anytime soon, not while Luke was in their territory. They knew they had the upper hand.

But Piper wasn't some weak women who would lie down and take this. All they'd done through the years was make her stronger. And Luke was hers. Hers to love and protect. Just like he'd protected her for months. She'd get him away from her parents and they'd live happily ever after.

Or that was her plan.

The trip to Blackwater territory didn't take long. Everyone was there, including the wolves from Big River, minus the babies. Everyone had the same look on their faces, the same one she was sure was on hers: anger and determination.

"Girl," Nova said, rushing to Piper as she stepped out of the truck. Her arms wrapped around her and hugged her tight. "We're going to get him back. I promise," she whispered into Piper's ear.

"I know," Piper whispered back, accepting the hug, pulling some strength from Nova.

All the women circled Piper, taking turns hugging her while the men stood back, their brows pulled low, their lips moving as they discussed plans so softly Piper could barely hear them.

Stepping closer to the guys, she smiled sadly as Colton reached his arms out to her. She stepped into his embrace but pulled away quickly. They were comforting her. She didn't want to be comforted. She wanted reassurance that Luke would be home tonight.

"When did this happen?" Piper asked.

They'd been together just hours ago. And then she'd gone shopping with her friends. They hadn't been out that long, had they?

"About two hours ago," Carter said.

All the bears were there, even the owner of the bar, Noah, and his mate Hollyn. Colton and Shawnee. Carter and June. And then all the wolves and their mates.

"Where are the pups?" Piper asked as she looked around.

"My dad's watching them. We wanted to help," Nova said, nodding to Lola.

"I'm so sorry," Lola said. "I swear we didn't know what was going on," she said.

"He's coming home," Peyton said as her eyes flared bright turquoise instead of the soft silvery blue of the rest of the wolves. "One way or another, your mate is coming home tonight."

Piper's eyes were wide. Was it so obvious to everyone that Luke and Piper were official? Neither of the had announced it, but they hadn't exactly hidden anything either.

"Why do you look surprised?" Peyton asked. Piper wasn't sure whether she was offended or curious.

"You all know we're mates? Like, true mates?" Piper asked.

"Girl. We can smell it on you. We can smell the change, even if we can't see the mark," Nova said, her eyes dropping to Piper's shoulder. "I assume he marked you like a cat?"

Piper's hand raised and covered the mark on the back of her neck. It tingled and throbbed lightly. But it was the best feeling in the world. She belonged to the man of her dreams, someone she was proud to call mate. She trusted him. She loved him.

And now he was in danger because of her.

This was what she'd been worried about all along. She'd feared Luke would put himself in front of a bullet for Piper. And he'd done that, figuratively. Even without talking to him or seeing him, Piper knew Barrett and the other men from her Pride had abused him, hurt him, made him sorry he'd ever met Piper.

No. She knew that last part wasn't true. She knew, no matter what happened to him, he would rather it be him taking the blows than Piper. As much as it tore her up inside. She'd give her life to have Luke at home, in his cabin, living his life before she ruined everything for him.

But they'd found happiness. And while that happiness might not be a long love story, it would be epic. At least to her it would be.

"So what are we going to do?" Piper asked, looking from one person to the next. There were so many people. There were sixteen of them. Seventeen if she counted herself. But would that be enough?

"I called my dad and asked for some help," Lola said. "He's still part of Reed's and my family Pack. The Alpha is a good guy. That's at least two more people. More if Koda can wrangle up a few more wolves."

"My sister wants to help," Eli said. "She's trying to convince a few of the other lionesses to join."

"I called the panthers but it went to voicemail," Gray said. He forced a smile. "The Ravenwood Pride are friends of ours. They've helped out a few other times. But they've been out of town for a while now." A few eyes turned to Hollyn, but Piper had enough to think about without worrying about Hollyn's story.

"I can't Shift, but I can still help," Hollyn said, holding her hand up as if she were in a classroom.

"Shawnee's out," Colton said.

"What?" the redhead almost screamed. "No way!"

"I agree with Colton," Carter said. "We can't risk the baby if it comes to a fight."

Piper discreetly glanced at Callie. She shook her head, letting Piper know she was in the clear. Not that it was a good thing she hadn't gotten pregnant yet. But if she was as fragile as Shawnee, and even if she hadn't told her mate yet, Piper would demand she stay back with Shawnee to stay safe.

"Okay. So we have sixteen counting Piper. We're not going to count the others until we know for sure," Carter said, running a hand down the back of his neck. He looked like he was fighting a Shift. Shoot. They all looked that way with their glowing eyes and the heavy scent of fur in the air.

Even she was fighting to keep her skin. But if it came to a fight, she'd let her cougar out to rip into anyone who dared lay a finger on her mate.

An hour and a half later, they had a plan. Piper was ready to scream with frustration at how calm everyone was being. Well. Not everyone. Micah had already Shifted once and gone after one of the other wolves. Peyton and Nova ended up having to Shift to break it up.

One look at Peyton's wolf and Piper understood why it'd been nicknamed *Cujo*. She was terrifying and a little out of control. But exactly what they'd need if it came to a battle. They just didn't have the numbers compared to the Pride. Hollyn kept trying to reassure Piper that she had something better than an animal inside of her, but Piper wasn't sure. She wasn't sure it was worth the possible injuries, or worse, the deaths of her new family and friends.

She could hand herself over to her parents and swear to whatever conditions they proposed. Then they'd release Luke and no one would get hurt.

As great as that sounded in her head, she knew the second they thought Piper was complacent, they'd kill Luke to teach her some sick, twisted lesson. The only way out of this was if they made Donnell Pride nervous. Would sixteen people do that?

"Dad's on his way over with Koda and three males from the Morse Pack," Lola said as she read a text.

"I heard from the panthers, but they're too far away. They're going to head this way, but it'll be a few hours before they make it," Gray said.

"We don't have a few hours," Piper whimpered.

"Luna and Amber are coming from Hope Pride," Eli said.

"That's twenty-three," Carter said, scratching at the stubble on his chin. "How many are in Donnell Pride, Piper?"

"It was around twenty-five when I was there. It could've grown by now."

"Twenty-three to twenty-five is really good odds," Carter said.

"Especially with *Cujo* and *Tinkerbell* over there," Nova said, jerking her head toward Hollyn.

"Your wolf is pretty mean, too," Emory said with a wink.

"So is Micah's. We've got a pretty big size advantage with the lions and bears," Callie said, looking at Piper and giving her a thumbs up. She had to be the sweetest one out of all of them.

Piper felt more confident with the bigger number. And Callie was right; the bears and lions would be quite a bit bigger than the cougars. She still hoped it didn't come to a fight. She'd hate to have to be the one to hurt her own flesh and blood, even if they'd never had a qualm about hurting her through the years.

Hours ago, Piper was worrying about what to get Luke for Christmas. Now, she was worried about whether they'd ever get a single Christmas together.

Chapter Twelve

Every inch of Luke's body ached to the point he was struggling to stay conscious. He had to, though. He had to keep his wits about him the best he could so he could find a fucking way out of this shit.

He should've known a piece of fucking of shit like Barrett wasn't honorable. He should've taken a couple of the guys with him to watch his back. He should've…

Shit.

By now, his Clan would have to know something was wrong. Piper would have to know. The sun had set over an hour ago. When Luke didn't show up at her door, Piper would start to worry. Even if no one had contacted her to let her know something had had happened, she'd know from his absence. She knew he'd never leave her alone. He'd always be there for her.

Although, if they kept with the fucking beatings, he might end up breaking the promise against his own will. How much could one man take before his body gave out? Those assholes had used their fists, feet, bats, anything they could get their hands on to hurt him.

He hadn't seen any women, but once they'd knocked him to the ground, he'd been dragged into the house where he was currently balled in the fetal position. No matter how many times he called to his bear, the asshole was a no show.

With a sigh, he mentally apologized to his animal. It wasn't his bear's fault; his body was too damaged for the Shift to take hold. He'd be in some weird, painful in between state until he was healed.

Part of Luke hoped his Clan was on their way to get him out of this fucking place. But the other part, the biggest part, hoped they weren't. Because he knew if they came here, Piper would be with them. No way could anything keep her away. That was a fact. Because it would be the same for him.

"Have you heard from her?" Luke heard a male say from somewhere in another part of the house.

"Not yet. She knows by now, though. Dad called the Alphas. Let them know that asshole in there was in the way of Pride business." That voice was the one and only Barrett. The same mother fucker who'd been beating on Piper when he'd found her.

Silence met his ears for a few beats. Then a deep sigh.

"This is screwed up, B. She's our sister. Why the hell are we going along with this?"

Okay. The other male was another of Piper's brothers. And he didn't sound happy about what was going on or how his sister was being treated.

"She has a duty just like any other broad in the Pride. She's skirting that duty, Josh."

"The laws changed over a year ago. She doesn't have to do that shit anymore. She can choose whether she wants to be with that prick, Andrew," Josh said. "And I don't blame her for not wanting him. He already has three mates. How many does he need? You really want our only sister to be some part of his harem?"

Barrett laughed. "Does it fucking matter how many mates he has? Dad ain't gonna be around forever. Andrew is this close to being Alpha. Wouldn't you rather our sister be mated to the Alpha over some bear?"

"Does it matter whether she's mated to an Alpha? Not like it'll give us any more power."

Luke sneered at the closed door. They were talking about their own blood as if she were a possession. Fuckers like those didn't deserve someone as wonderful and sweet as Piper in their family.

Pushing onto his elbows, Luke bit back the groan as he felt bones sliding into place as they healed. How many breaks did he have? And were they just giving him time to heal before they came back in for round…fuck…how many rounds had it been? He'd lost count a long fucking time ago. Around the same time he'd felt a few ribs crack and searing pain rocket through his system.

He needed to find a way out of this place. Or find a phone and contact Carter or Colton. Someone. Anyone. He needed to make sure they kept Piper as far away from her family Pride as possible.

"Shh," someone said. "You hear that?" Josh this time.

"Trucks. A few of them. I told you her dumbass would come home if we took her boyfriend," Barrett said. A clap sounded and Luke could picture Barrett patting his brother Josh on the back, a wide, stupid grin on his stupid fucking face.

Steps pounded through the house, a door opened and closed, and then muffled voices sounded outside the window. He must be in a room close to the front of the house because he could hear more people talking outside, could hear the vehicles pulling up the paved driveway. Several trucks. If Piper was there, she'd brought an army with her.

Pride struck him as he pictured his mate stepping from one of the vehicles, her chin raised, all of their friends stretching behind and beside her. They'd tried to create a victim. All they'd done was form a warrior. His warrior.

"Where is he?" Piper called out.

"He's safe," Barrett said.

"Come on over here," a woman said. "And the bear can go home."

"I'm not here to stay, mom," Piper said.

Okay. So there were females around even though Luke hadn't seen any.

"Go get him," the woman said.

A door opened. Closed. Feet thundered quickly down the hall toward Luke. He was yanked off the mattress with rough hands and dragged through the house. He tried and failed to get his feet under him, to walk on his own. More broken bones in his lower half.

Straining to open his eyes, he lifted his head and hissed through his teeth when the asshole on his left wrenched his head up further by a handful of hair.

"Stop!" Piper screamed. No. Not screamed. Ordered. Luke knew he looked as shitty as he felt. Yet his mate was standing tall, her jaw set, her feet shoulder width apart. And she wasn't alone.

Every single person from Big River Pack and Blackwater Clan was there. No. Shawnee was missing. Good. A possible fight with a Pride of cruel cougars was too risky for a pregnant Shifter. Especially a lioness. No telling how many cubs were in her belly or even what kind.

Luke's head dropped forward when his hair was released. Slowly and with a crap ton of effort, he raised it again to watch his warrior mate. He'd thought of her that way before. Now, she looked the fucking part.

"You're awful brave today," Barrett said from Luke's left. He'd moved closer, like he was trying to intimidate either Piper or Luke. Luke sure as fuck wasn't intimidated by the piece of shit. And, although Luke had seen a hint of fear in Piper's eyes as they darted to Luke's face then back to her brother, she kept her chin raised, her shoulders back, and her brows furrowed.

"I've always been brave, asshole," Piper said, a sarcastic smirk pulling up one side of her mouth. "Why do you think I haven't come back here? You are nothing to me. None of you are," she said, looking at her brothers, her parents, the Pride members who were gathering around to watch or lend a hand. Luke wasn't sure which and, apparently, Piper and the rest of his people weren't either. And they looked like they didn't give a shit which.

"How dare you come here and talk to us like that," Piper's mom said, taking a slow step forward.

Peyton matched her slow step, her eyes bright turquoise as she fought her crazy ass wolf for control. If one of these people Shifted, Peyton's wolf would burst through and go for blood. It was obvious she'd already taken Piper in as part of her personal Pack, even if Piper would technically be a Blackwater Clan member. But *Cujo*, as Nova had so lovingly nicknamed the psychotic animal, didn't care about logistics. She cared about her people.

Piper's mom's eyes darted to Peyton and narrowed. "Do you think any of your little friends hold any power here? Do you really think the Donnell Pride fears any of you?" she said, looking over the people standing behind and beside Piper.

"Sure look scared to me," Peyton said, her voice full of her animal's growl.

As happy as he was to see everyone, as happy as he was to see his mate standing up for herself and for him, Luke didn't want this to come to a fight. He didn't want Piper or any of them to get hurt because of him. This was his fault. He knew better. He'd let emotion take over and threw caution to the wind. He could find a way out himself without any bloodshed.

But Piper had other ideas. She mimicked Peyton and took a step closer, her eyes locked on her mother's. "I think you've feared me my whole life. Why else would you try so hard to beat me down? Why else would you try to turn me into something weak and pathetic? News flash, mom: it didn't work. No matter how many times you send Barret or anyone else to slap me around, it will never work." Piper's head tilted to the side a little. "I guess I should thank you."

"For what?" Piper's mother said, her lips quivering. Oh yeah. She was scared, even if she didn't want to show it.

"For making me stronger. For helping me to appreciate real love and real friendships. For showing me how much power I have."

"Power," her mother spat. "What kind of power do you have? You're a skinny, weird, mousy thing who couldn't even land a cougar. You had to sink so low as to take a bear as a mate."

Piper's lips pulled up in a slow smile. "The power to make you nervous. The power to back your own Pride down." Her eyes raised over her mother's head.

Luke turned his head the same time Piper's mother looked behind her. Half of Donnell Pride was slowly backing away, their eyes bouncing over the Blackwater Clan, Big River Pack, members of Hope Pride and Morse Pack. They were only outnumbered by a few, but there was an intensity in all their eyes, a promise of violence in pain if things didn't go the way Piper wanted.

When Piper's mother turned back, her eyes were wider, her lips quivered harder. "I'm your mother. You're supposed to show me some respect."

"Respect is earned, mom. If you want my respect, you'll have to earn it. And you can start by releasing my mate…with an apology."

Her mother snorted derisively and rolled her eyes. But then she looked to her eldest son Barret with question in her eyes.

"You can't be serious," Barret said. "If we take this bastard out, she'll have to come home. You promised Andrew. Dad promised Andrew."

Luke frowned. Piper's father stood beside his wife with his arms crossed over his chest, a deep scowl on his older face, but he hadn't said a word. He'd let his wife and son take over the meeting. What kind of Alpha didn't control his own Pride? What kind of Alpha…

Luke focused harder; her dad looked frail, thin, and was swaying slightly on his feet. He was sick. He was trying to force his daughter into mating the male he chose so she would be part of the family who took over his Pride when he either couldn't any more or when he died.

Part of Luke felt for her dad. But the bigger part, the part who refused to allow women to be treated as anything less than queens, hated him for it. Sick or not, he should allow the stronger male to become Alpha and allow not just his daughter, but all the women in the Pride to choose their own mates, allow them to find their true mates.

Luke straightened, his spine bowing in pain as bones glided back into place. But he kept his mouth shut, swallowing the bellow of pain and did his best to keep it off his face. He needed Piper to focus on the possible threat in front of her, not his injuries. They'd heal with time.

"If anyone touches my mate, I will personally rip your throat out, Barrett. I'm not scared of you. Not anymore. In fact, you're pathetic. What kind of man assaults a woman half his size? All that tells me is you can't fight anyone your own size." Piper took another step forward. "I meant what I said. You are nothing to me. After today, I'm going to forget you exist. I have a new family. And they're all that matters to me. Not your backward plans for my future. Not your forced slavery. Not any of it."

She moved forward until she was touching distance from Luke with Peyton and Colton on her heels. No one moved closer to her. No one threatened her or Luke. There weren't a whole lot of Pride members left to back the Alpha and his family.

"We're going home. And none of you will contact me again." Piper looped an arm through Luke's. Colton stepped up to his other side and helped him to the group of people waiting. "You will never contact me again," Piper repeated, locking eyes with each of her parents, then her brothers, leaving Barrett for last. "If you ever show up at my house again, I'm going to let my mate rip you to shreds."

The scent of fur was strong in the circle of his people. But their presence lent him strength and he was able to walk on his own with a little support from Colton and Carter.

Piper gave her former Pride, her former family her back as she walked away, leading Luke and everyone else away and toward their trucks. The second they were out of sight of the cougars, Piper's façade cracked beside Luke.

First her bottom lip quivered. Then tears welled and spilled over her lashes, streaking down her cheeks. She gently leaned against Luke's shoulder and wept silently. "I'm so sorry," she whispered. "This is my fault."

Luke grunted in pain when Carter's truck hit a bump. "No, it's not," he gritted through his teeth. "This is on me."

Piper dragged both hands down her face, wiping the tears away. "Oh, I'm definitely mad at you, too. But if you hadn't tried to save me from my own life, you wouldn't be sitting here looking…" Her eyes trailed over Luke from head to toe. "Like you just went three rounds with Mike Tyson."

"It's not that bad," he said, hiding the grimace as the truck dropped into a pothole.

****

Piper's heart hurt. Luke sat beside her in Carter's truck, every muscle tense as Carter slowly navigated the vehicle over the bumpy road as they headed home. Her mate was covered in bruises from head to toe. Both eyes were swollen almost shut, his face was smeared with blood, and she could tell by the way he gritted his teeth and bowed his back that several broken bones were healing themselves.

He was trying so hard to hide it from her. But she could tell. And it hurt her heart even more that, even in immense pain, he was trying to protect Piper. It was her turn to keep him safe.

"I should've kicked his butt," Piper whispered as another round of tears threatened to spill over her lashes.

"Who?" Luke grunted out. The bumpy road finally gave way to the smooth highway. But they'd end up jostling him again when they hit the gravel of the Clan's long driveway.

"Barrett! I should've marched right up to him and punched him in his stupid face," Piper said, shaking her fist in the air.

Luke snorted, his lips curled up at the corners, but then grimaced in pain. "You're so damn cute," he said, his voice closer to a groan than a growl.

Piper knew from experience the kind of damage her brothers had inflicted on Luke would take days to heal. That would be days of pain for her mate. Because of her.

But maybe Luke had been right. None of this was her fault. She hadn't asked to be treated the way she had been her whole life. She hadn't asked Luke to step in and defend her. She hadn't asked him to camp out in her yard every night. Those were other people's choices.

From that day on, she'd choose to be happy. She'd choose to forget those people, forget the abuse they'd tortured her with, forget a life before Luke and her new family existed.

Just as she'd feared, the long, bumpy, gravel driveway to Blackwater territory jostled Luke and caused him pain.

"Brother, I can stop here and carry you the rest of the way," Carter offered, frowning in the rearview mirror.

"I'm fine," Luke said, his teeth clenched so hard Piper could see the muscles of his jaw working.

With a nod, Carter continued toward the cabins, pulling up directly alongside Luke's so he wouldn't have so far to walk.

Everyone was there, waiting for him at the bottom of the steps. Colton and Carter moved to each side of him and helped him up the stairs while Piper led the way, pushing open his door. She'd never been to his cabin, had no idea where his bedroom was.

As she stood and watched the men help Luke down the hall, Piper took a second to look around the cozy space. It was dark, the wood of his cabin exposed and uncovered by drywall or paint. It was kind of messy, too, but not dirty. And it smelled so much like him her heart fluttered. There were books all over the coffee table, movie cases lying on the floor in front of the massive flat screen TV. But the floor was clean and the kitchen just off the living room was tidy except for the coffee mug sitting in the sink.

For some reason, she'd expected his house to be chaotic. Instead it was homey and sort of relaxed Piper.

Had she ever been relaxed in her own home? She loved her house, loved her furniture, but she wasn't sure she'd ever actually been able to be at peace.

Piper jogged to catch up with the guys and stood beside the bed, looking down at Luke. "Can I get you something? Are you hungry?"

"Always trying to feed me," Luke said with a chuckle, then winced at the pain it brought him. By the way he was holding his side, Piper guessed he had a few cracked ribs on top of everything else.

A new rush of rage hit her system. Why the hell hadn't she punished Barrett while she'd been there? She should've Shifted and attacked him, gotten her pound of flesh, avenged her mate. But if she'd Shifted, so would her family Pride. Then her new friends would've Shifted and war would've ensued. It was bad enough Luke was suffering; she couldn't stand the thought of anyone else getting hurt, too.

"I'll get him some water," Shawnee said from the doorway. She must've been going nuts waiting for all of them to return with Luke.

Her footsteps were almost silent as she hurried from the room. The three bears of Blackwater were hovering near the bed. Piper could hear everyone else in the hallway and in the living room, waiting to find out if Luke was okay.

"We'll give you some time. Either of you let us know if you need anything at all. I'll make sure there's some easy to make food in your fridge for the next few days," Carter said as he pushed from the dresser with a nod.

"Thank you," Piper said around a lump in her throat.

Easy to make food. Because Carter knew how hard it would be for Piper to leave Luke's side while he was healing. She still couldn't believe he'd risked his life to fight for her freedom. He'd literally put himself in the line of fire to shield her, to keep anyone who meant her harm out of her life. And she'd spend the rest of her life showing him how much that meant to her and how grateful she was to have him.

Lowering carefully on to the side of the bed, Piper stared down at Luke as tears welled in her eyes once again.

"Stop looking at me like I'm dying. I'll be fine. Just give me a minute," Luke said, reaching out and taking her hand in his. Even that small movement seemed to cause him pain and made Piper angry and crushed at the same time.

"I wish I could take the pain away," Piper whispered, slowly lowering to lie beside Luke, keeping his hand in hers. She had a hard time pulling her eyes from him, as if he'd disappear if he was no longer in her sight.

"I'm fine. Stop worrying about me."

"I can't believe you did that," she whispered. Soft footsteps were moving around Luke's house and through his front door. Piper could hear quiet conversation outside his cabin, but their voices were too low for her to make out exactly what they were saying.

"I'd do anything for you. I hope you know that. I'd go through a hundred beatings if it meant you were free."

Piper could no longer hold back the tears. They streamed from her eyes to soak into her hair and the pillow below her head. "I know." She sniffled and touched his cheek gingerly. "I love you, Luke."

"I love you, too. So much," he said barely above a breath as his eyes fluttered closed and his breathing became even.

He needed sleep. He needed rest to heal. And Piper stayed right where she was, staring at him until the sky outside the window turned a hazy gray with the sunrise. Only then did her eyes grow heavy and sleep dragged her under. Even then, she kept a tight grasp on Luke's hand, her other hand resting on his chest so she could feel it raise and lower with each breath to assure herself he was still there, still breathing, still alive.

Chapter Thirteen

It had taken a full week for Luke to heal enough to be able to get out of bed and move around on his own. Piper had stayed by his side, only leaving long enough to relieve herself in the bathroom, take quick showers, and make him food. She finally got the opportunity to cook for him and he'd devoured it with enthusiasm.

"I can't believe I've been missing out this whole time," he'd said.

Now, she laid in his bed, itching for him to wake up so they could have their first Christmas together.

Since she hadn't wanted to leave Luke's side, she'd sent the women on a mission for her. She'd decided just slapping a bow on her body as a gift could never be enough, not after he'd almost died to give her her life back. And although what she'd asked the ladies to find for her wasn't nearly as big as his gift had been, it was the best she could do being as she'd never given a gift to anyone before.

They hadn't left Luke's house and he didn't have a tree up. Piper had tried to give Nova some money to find a small tree for his house, but she'd refused. She'd said it gave her another way to spend her money on her family.

After a few FaceTime calls, the girls had found the perfect gift, wrapped it for Piper, and delivered it last night…on Christmas Eve. It sat under a six-foot tree fully decorated by every single female in her life. They'd been as quiet as they could, but Piper was sure Luke had heard them in his living room and knew something was up. He'd never said anything, never let on that he knew Piper was planning a surprise.

Finally, after what felt like forever, Luke's lashes fluttered and his eyes opened to find Piper sitting up against the headboard watching him.

"I'd say that's creepy, but I've watched you sleep a few times, too," Luke said with a stretch. His bones had healed and all the swelling had gone down, but there were still some gray, brown, and green bruises across his face and the rest of his body. Stupid Barrett. And stupid whoever else helped beat on her mate.

"You want breakfast before Christmas starts?" Piper asked, unable to hold back her excitement any longer.

"Pretty sure Christmas started at midnight," Luke said as he sat up and threw his legs over the side of the bed.

Piper's eyes roamed Luke's shoulders and back. Even marred with scars and bruises, the sight of him still warmed her body in ways nothing else ever could. She couldn't wait until he was healed enough to make love again. She felt like she was going through withdrawals in the week since they'd last been intimate.

Luke looked at Piper over his shoulder. "You look excited," he said, his smile widening into a grin.

He stood and rounded the bed, stopping in front of her to pull her to her feet. He cupped her cheeks in both strong hands, dipped his head and touched his lips to hers. She'd brushed her teeth already, so she didn't push him away like she normally would have. She was pretty sure she'd never push him away again, not after coming so close to losing him permanently.

"Come on," he said, taking her hand in his and pulling her from the bedroom.

He stopped at the end of the hallway and stared at the tree. "I was wondering what was going on out here last night," he said with a wink down at Piper. "Is that the one from your house?" he asked.

"No. Nova wanted to get one for your house, too."

"*Our* house. Whether you ever live here with me or not, this is your home, too," he said, his face going all serious.

Piper did everything she could to keep the smile off her face as she nodded. She knew Luke wanted her to live with him in his cabin. She knew he wanted her in his home and surrounded by his Clan. And now, she was even more excited for him to open his gift.

"You first," he said, guiding her to the couch and urging her to sit. The only gifts under the tree were from her, so she was confused. He was supposed to have gone shopping with the girls the day he'd been attacked by Piper's former Pride, but he'd never made it. And he'd been in bed ever since.

Piper frowned as Luke headed toward the front door, stepped outside, and came back in with wrapped boxes and gift bags. There were so many. And all she had were the three for him sitting under the tree and some small stuff in the stocking hanging over the fireplace. Piper had been confused as to why anyone would put candy and gifts in a sock, but the women had told her it was tradition.

Setting everything at Piper's feet, Luke carefully lowered onto the cushion beside her and watched her expectantly.

"There are so many," Piper said, again looking at her meager gifts under the tree and wondering if it would be enough.

"Not nearly enough. But it was the best I could do from bed."

He'd had Nova or one of the other women help, just like she had. But when? When was he able to communicate with them since she was always by his side? Must have been when she was showering or cooking for him. Kind of like she'd texted and talked while he slept or showered.

Piper lifted the first box into her lap and slowly pulled the wrapping paper away.

"You gotta rip into it, baby," Luke said with one of his heart stopping grins.

Rip into it. Okay. A little chaotic for her, but he seemed excited by the idea. So, she grabbed a spot and tore at the paper. It was a brown, cardboard box with no label on it. No clues. Setting it at her feet, she tore the tape away and peered inside.

He'd bought her an organizing basket, one of those pretty kinds she'd always admired. "Wow! Thanks," she said, pulling it out and inspecting it. She already knew exactly what she'd use it for.

Box after box, bag after bag, Piper found more organizing stuff, cleaning tools, and a new sweater, similar to the cardigans she usually wore, only this one was definitely better quality. He'd bought her things he knew she'd want and love. He'd put thought into her gifts, even if they were things he'd never want or use himself. He knew exactly what would make her happy.

"Thank you so much," she said after setting down the sweater. She held up her arms and sighed when he leaned into her hug, wrapping his big, strong arms around her back and holding her for a few seconds.

Finally pulling away, Piper leapt to her feet and hurried to the tree. "Now you're turn," she said, carrying the boxes over to where Luke waited. She set them on the coffee table, then sat and watched him anxiously.

What if her gift wasn't as exciting as she'd built in her head? What if she'd read him wrong? What if he hated what she'd given him?

Luke did like he'd told her and ripped the paper away from the box. He peered inside and frowned when he spotted the suitcase. Piper didn't say a word, just let him move onto the next box. That one held a picture of the entire crew – minus Piper – that said *Family* in a pretty font on the frame.

The last box was thin and long. He frowned down at the papers until he comprehended what he was looking at. His eyes went wide as he slowly turned them to Piper.

"I sold my house. That's the contract. Someone bought it the second day it was listed." Luke still didn't say anything, just continued to stare at Piper. "I mean, if you think I should stay there, I still have time to back out. The closing isn't until –"

Piper's words were cut off by Luke's lips slamming down on hers, the box with the thick stack of legal documents tossed onto the coffee table so he could wrap his arms around her and drag her close.

For the first time in a week, Piper and Luke were able to make love. This time it was tender instead of desperate and hungry. Every touch, every caress, every thrust of Luke's hips held so much emotion Piper didn't bother fighting it as tears slipped from the corners of her eyes to soak into her hair.

As they lie on the couch, Luke still cradled between her thighs, his lips pressing sweet kisses against hers, Piper realized she literally held her entire world in her arms. Never would anyone ever be as happy, content, and blessed as she was at that very moment.

Luke had not only woken her heart, he'd freed her from the chains her family tried to force on her, he'd given her a new family, he'd shown her love and how good life could really be.

He'd given her everything.

"I love you, Luke," she whispered against his lips.

He pulled back and looked into her eyes, the amber glow bright in his whiskey colored irises. "I love you so much. Never doubt that, my little warrior."

And just like in the ending of every single one of the romance books she'd devoured, Piper and Luke lived happily ever after.

####

If you enjoyed Luke's Redemption, Lynn would be over the moon if you left a review on Amazon and/or Goodreads..

About the Author

Lynn Howard lives in Cedar Hill, MO, where all her sexy Shifters exist. She lives and breathes hot Alpha males and sassy brassy females. She feels the most at home knee deep in mud and chicken muck and prefers to be outside under the stars, cuddled up under a blanket in front of a bonfire than in the big city.

When not typing away or feeding her chickens, you can find her fantasizing about hot country boys for her next book or wandering the woods in search of wildlife. She loves all animals and insects...except spiders. Her favorite foot accessory is barefoot and she owns at least twenty sets of salt-n-pepper shakers, yet only uses one.

Gray's Wolf is the first in the Big River Pack series. And just like in Gray's Wolf, there are more hot country boy Shifters just waiting to their turn for a little love and romance.

Character Index

Big River Pack
Grayson (Gray) Harvey – Alpha – wolf
Micah Matthews– Second – wolf/coyote hybrid
Reed Peterson – wolf
Tristan – wolf
Peyton Mathes – wolf – mate to Tristan
Nova Harvey – wolf – mate to Gray
Callie Taylor – mate to Micah
Lola Braun – wolf – Reed's mate

Blackwater Clan
Carter – bear
Colton Barnes – bear
Luke – bear
Noah – bear – owner of Moe's Tavern
Shawnee Baker aka Fancy Pants – lioness – mate to Colton
Hollyn – Elemental Fae – Noah's mate
Piper – cougar – new mate to Luke

Ravenwood Pride
Aron – Alpha – panther
Mason – panther
Brax – panther – brother to Daxon
Daxon – panther – brother to Brax

Deathport Pack
~~Anson – Alpha – wolf~~
Felix – New Alpha – wolf
Barrett – wolf
Kaleb – wolf
Tanner – wolf

Tammen Pride
~~Rhett – Alpha – lion~~
Trever – lion
~~Brent – lion~~
Brian – lion
Chuck – lion – owner of Dodson's Garage

Council Members
Alan Price – wolf - Nova's biological dad
~~Frank – wolf – Colton's dad~~

Hope Pride
Eli – lion - Alpha
Emory – wolf – Eli's mate
Luna – lioness – sister to Eli
Amber – lioness
Petra – lioness

Remsen Pride
~~Jace – lion – Emory's former mate~~

Morse Pack
Eric Branes – wolf – Second
Koda – Alpha
Carl Braun – wolf – Lola's dad

Made in the USA
Middletown, DE
11 May 2021